PURRFECT SPARKLE

THE MYSTERIES OF MAX 37

NIC SAINT

PURRFECT SPARKLE

The Mysteries of Max 37

Copyright © 2021 by Nic Saint

All rights reserved. No part of this book may be reproduced in any form by any electronic or mechanical means including photocopying, recording, or information storage and retrieval without permission in writing from the author.

This is a work of fiction. Names, characters, places, brands, media, and incidents are either the product of the author's imagination or are used fictitiously. The author acknowledges the trademarked status and trademark owners of various products referenced in this work of fiction, which have been used without permission. The publication/use of these trademarks is not authorized, associated with, or sponsored by the trademark owners.

Edited by Chereese Graves

www.nicsaint.com

Give feedback on the book at: info@nicsaint.com

facebook.com/nicsaintauthor
@nicsaintauthor

First Edition

Printed in the U.S.A

1

"Max?"

"Mh?"

"Do you think the earth is round… or flat?"

I opened one lazy eye and instructed it to take in my friend Dooley, who was lying right next to me on the lawn. "Why do you ask?"

"Well, I was talking to Buster last night, and he told me that Fido has become a member of the Flat Earth Society. And now Buster is wondering if his human is off his rocker, or if he's onto something. And since he knows I'm a specialist, he decided to ask me for advice."

"You're a specialist?" I asked, quirking an amused eyebrow.

"Well, everyone knows that I watch the Discovery Channel, Max, which makes me a specialist in pretty much everything. So they all come to me with the tough questions." He made a face. "Though I have to admit that even with all of that knowledge under my belt, some of these questions still get me stumped, like now with Buster."

I yawned and stretched out on the smooth lawn. Ever

since Chase decided to borrow his father-in-law's lawn-mower from time to time, he kept the lawn manicured to perfection, almost like a golf course. And he wasn't getting any complaints from me. I like those golf course lawns: smooth like a billiard table, with no excess blades of grass tickling those sensitive body parts.

"So what do you think, Max?" Dooley insisted. "Flat or round?"

"Hasn't there been a documentary about the Flat Earth Society recently?" I asked, not in the mood for this philosophical stuff. When the sun is tickling my belly, and I'm on the verge of diving headfirst into a relaxing slumber, the kind of slumber that refreshes and makes you feel like a new cat, I try to avoid interruptions that will stand in the way of the perfect napping experience.

"I don't think so," said my friend, frowning. "Unless I missed something." His eyes went wide. "Oh, no, Max! Maybe I missed this all-important documentary! Now I'm suffering from POMO!"

"It's FOMO, Dooley, not POMO."

"No, definitely POMO. Pair of missing out."

"That makes no sense at all."

"Oh, it does, Max. You see, if you miss out once, it's fine, but if you miss out twice, it's bad. So a pair of missing out, see?"

All I saw was that my friend had been misinformed, either by some joker who was pulling his paw, or with good intentions. But since I was too relaxed to bother, I decided not to engage.

Dooley is a gray raggamuffin, by the way, and a good deal smaller than myself. I'm a tabby with fur the color of the setting sun. I call it blorange, a contraction of blond and orange, though there have been folks who don't always see the distinction and simply call me orange. I'm what you might call a full-bodied cat, on account of the fact that I was born with big bones. Don't let my sizable appearance fool you, though. I'm generally a sweet-natured feline, not inclined to cause bodily harm to anyone, man or beast, unless they try to cause me harm first, of course, and even then.

"I think the answer is very simple, Dooley."

"It is?"

"Sure. Tell Buster to start walking in any direction, and just keep on walking. If after a while he falls off the face of the planet, the earth is flat. If he ends up back where he started, it's round. Easy peasy."

Dooley thought about this for a moment, which gave me the opportunity to drift off into the refreshing sleep I just mentioned. Unfortunately, just when I was about to plunge headfirst into oblivion, he spoke once more.

"I think that's brilliant, Max."

"Of course it is," I said, deciding not to bother with humility for once.

"I'll tell him tonight, and he can start his experiment immediately."

"You do that," I murmured, the warmth of the sun now having a profoundly soporific effect on me.

For a long moment, things were quiet there in Odelia's backyard. Odelia Poole is my human, and Chase Kingsley her husband. Together they take good care of us, and in return we take good care of them. The perfect example of you scratch my back and I'll scratch yours, though it's easier for them—and less painful—to scratch my back than it is for me to scratch theirs.

"Max?" suddenly my friend piped up again.

I released a tired sigh. "Dooley?"

"So I was thinking, maybe we can join Buster on his trip."

"What trip?" I asked, having long forgotten the topic of our recent conversation.

"Why, his trip around the world, of course. We start off here, and we just keep on walking until we get back where we took off, and that way we'll have settled once and for all that the earth is round, not flat, like Fido seems to think."

"I don't think that's such a good idea, Dooley," I said, this time not even bothering to open my peepers.

"Oh, and why is that?"

"For one thing, the earth is very, very big, and for another, how are we going to survive, traipsing all around the globe without our daily dose of kibble?"

"We could ask Odelia to prepare us a snack?"

I smiled at my friend's naivety. He may watch the Discovery Channel on a regular basis, but that doesn't mean he's wise to the ways of the world yet.

"Dooley, do you have any idea how long it would take us to travel all around the world?"

"Um… a day? Maybe two?"

"At the rate of speed we travel, it will probably take us a couple of years."

"Years!"

"Sure. Like I said, the world is a big place, Dooley, and we're small in comparison."

"Oh," he said, his excitement somewhat dampened. But if I thought he'd give up now, I was of course mistaken, as I should have foreseen. Once my friend gets a thought into his tiny nut, it's very hard to dislodge it, even with the assistance of a monkey wrench. Or a cat wrench, if such a device exists.

"So what if we ask Odelia to come along with us? She has a car, and that way it won't take us years but maybe just a couple of days, right?"

"Even if Odelia took us along in her car, it would still take us months to travel around the world," I said. "Also, since a large portion of the earth is covered in oceans, we'd need to swim across those oceans. And I don't think Odelia will be up for such a challenge." I knew I wasn't. Wild horses couldn't drag me away from the small town I like to call home—or even tame ones.

"So... what if Odelia and Chase built a boat, and we traveled across those oceans by boat?" He shivered at the thought. Cats aren't entirely fond of traveling in a small metal box that bobs up and down on the waves. We'd recently allowed Odelia and Chase to drag us along on their honeymoon, which they'd chosen to spend on a cruise ship, and we still hadn't fully recovered from the ordeal.

"Look, Odelia has a job, and so does Chase," I pointed out. "Their respective bosses aren't going to allow them to go on some crazy trip trying to prove what everyone already knows to be true anyway."

"And what's that?" Dooley asked, interested.

"That the earth is round!"

"Fido doesn't seem to think so."

"That's because Fido is an idiot," I said, starting to lose my patience.

"So... the earth isn't flat?" asked Dooley, just to make sure.

"No, it's not. And now can I please take my nap? Thank you."

For a while, things were pleasantly quiet. Birds were chirping in the background, crickets were rubbing their wings, and I was about to engage in a kibble-filled dream when Dooley said, "Or we could ask Odelia to charter a plane. If we don't fly too high, and keep an eye on the ground, we'll know when we reach the world's edge, wouldn't we?"

"There is no edge," I said.

"I know, and that's what we need to prove to Fido. So we'll take him along in our plane so he can see for himself."

"Honestly? I really don't care what Fido thinks."

"But Buster does. He's really worried about him."

"Worried in what sense?"

"Well, he's online all the time, talking to his flat earth friends, and he's been neglecting his business, except when he's trying to convince his customers about some of his ideas. They're already starting to go elsewhere for their haircuts."

"Fido is losing customers?"

"In droves, Max. The talk in town is that you can't get a haircut without having Fido trying to fill your head with all kinds of nonsense, and who needs that?"

I certainly didn't. Then again, I'm not the kind of cat who likes to go to the hair salon, so I can't really speak from experience. But the Pooles are all very fond of Fido, especially the ladies. Odelia visits him once a month, her mom Marge twice a month and Gran even schedules weekly visits to make sure her little white curls are always in tip-top shape. The men are a different story. Uncle Alec never goes, since one of the requirements of going to a hair salon is that you actually have hair on top of your head, which I'm sorry to say is not so much the case anymore for Odelia's uncle. His girlfriend Charlene Butterwick, our local mayor, doesn't seem to mind, though. She herself is an avid Fido fan, and then there are Odelia's dad Tex, who's a lukewarm salon goer, as is Chase.

Chase is a cop, you see, and cops, since they are in constant contact with the members of the public, need to look presentable to some extent, so as not to scare them off too much. And Tex Poole is a doctor, and no sick person likes to visit a doctor who looks like a hell's angel.

"So maybe we'll drop by the hair salon later," I told my friend. In spite of myself, this whole Flat Earth Society business had piqued my curiosity, and I wanted to see firsthand what effect Fido's affiliation was having on the man's state of mind. If he was scaring off his clientele, maybe Dooley and Buster were right, and something needed to be done. Hair hygiene is a serious business, and if Fido scared away all of his customers, soon Hampton Cove would turn into a hippie town, where the greasy mane ruled supreme.

Though to be perfectly honest I didn't see how three cats could possibly be instrumental in rectifying this situation. It's hard to make humans change their minds about something once an idea has taken root in those big noggins they precariously balance on their necks. And I may be a lot of things but I'm not a shrink, so I wouldn't know how to treat delusional behavior even if I tried.

Still, Buster was our good friend, and so it behooved us to try and find a way to help him in his hour of need.

2

Odelia Poole sat hunched over her small desk, frowning at the screen of her laptop computer. From time to time she glanced up to look out the window, which offered a view of the backyard of her own house and that of the neighboring houses. It had been Chase's idea to install this modest office for her, so she could work from home when she wanted to. And it certainly was a very pleasant little space, located in the bedroom. Before it had been turned into an office it had been a spacious closet, but since Odelia wasn't a beauty queen or felt the need to spend her hard-earned cash on fancy outfits, she'd used it as storage space, and a place to store her ironing board. On Chase's instigation they'd relegated most of the stuff to the attic or Goodwill, and while Chase and Tex put up some shelves, Odelia and her mom had gone shopping for a nice desk, a decent office chair and even an armchair where she could think and thresh out ideas—if her cats allowed her to use it, of course, since they'd discovered the space, too—and loved it!

"Diamonds, diamonds, diamonds..." she murmured as

she intently gazed at her screen. "Bring me your diamonds, good sir or madam, whether they be white, pink, yellow, orange or black."

Lately a peculiar story had developed right in the heart of Hampton Cove. A little girl collecting seashells on the beach had picked up what looked like a sparkling piece of glass, and had excitedly handed it to her mommy, who was reading a book nearby. The piece of glass had looked too polished to be part of a broken bottle, and when the woman had studied the item more closely, she'd discovered that it was very nicely cut like a gemstone of some kind.

So she'd taken it into town to a local jeweler to have it looked at, and the jeweler's jaw had practically dropped to the floor when he indulgently studied what he figured was a piece of colored glass with his loupe, and had discovered that it was a flawless pink diamond of exquisite cut, and probably worth a small fortune.

Of course the news had traveled fast, and plenty of people had soon taken up vigil on the beach, looking for more diamonds where that first one had come from.

The police had gotten involved when the jeweler had declared the stone to be of extreme value, and the hunt was on to find its owner. Oddly enough, no one came forward to claim the stone.

Odelia's editor, who smelled a great article, had put his star reporter on the story. And since it wasn't inconceivable that the stone had been accidentally dropped there by thieves, Odelia had been scouring the web in search of stories of people having been robbed of such a valuable gem. She leaned back when she realized that she was suffering from that typical malady of your intrepid journo: she didn't have enough information to write a decent piece. Yet. An omission that could easily be remedied by going into town and finding out what she needed to know.

And it was with the kind of swiftness and alacrity typical of the dynamic young woman that she was, that she rose from her chair, closed her laptop, tucked it into her shoulder bag, then lightly darted down the stairs and out the door. She paused on the threshold, though, and smiled as she retraced her steps.

Crossing over to the sliding glass door, she opened it and called out, "Max, Dooley—I'm hunting down a story. Wanna join me?"

And it was a testament to her two cats' spirit of adventure that they didn't need to be told twice.

Immediately both cats came tripping up to her, looking eager to partake in her latest adventure.

"What is it?" asked Dooley excitedly. "Are you going to try to prove that the earth is round?"

She laughed at that. "Now why would I want to prove something that's a known fact, honey? No, I want to talk to a jeweler."

"A jeweler?" asked the small gray cat. "Are you going to buy a ring?"

"Not exactly," she said as she headed out the door, her two cats in tow. "I need to ask him a couple of questions about a diamond that was found on the beach yesterday."

"Diamonds!" said Dooley, his eyes shining as brightly as she imagined that diamond had shone.

"Diamond, singular," she said as she held open the door of her aged pickup truck, to allow both cats to hop up onto the backseat. She closed the door, and assumed her position behind the wheel. "Though of course where there's one diamond, there may be others."

"Cool!" said Dooley, who never stinted for pretty excitement and youthful zeal.

Max, more laidback and assuming the attitude of an elder

statesman, said, "Is this the diamond nobody knows the origin of?"

"Yep. They call it the Pink Lady."

She started up her engine, and soon was tootling along the road into town.

"Why do they call it that, Odelia?" asked Dooley.

"Well, mainly because it's pink, I guess," she said, "and also because it looks exactly like a famous diamond called the Pink Lady."

It had actually been Dolores Peltz, the police station dispatcher, who thought she recognized the gem when Dan had published a picture on the Gazette website. This particular diamond had been set in an engagement ring, offered by Sheikh Bab El Ehr, ruler of Khemed, to his betrothed on the occasion of their marriage. The gem had gone missing thirty-something years ago, never to be found.

"Did the Pink Lady belong to a real pink lady?" asked Dooley.

"I doubt it, Dooley. Besides, chances that this diamond is the actual Pink Lady are very slim."

"So it could be *a* pink lady, but not *the* Pink Lady?"

"Exactly," she said with a smile as she parked her car in front of Gems World, the jeweler on whose shoulders now rested the responsibility of finding out where this diamond came from.

3

*T*hormond Linoski, owner and proprietor of Gems World ('A World of Gems at Your Fingertips'), was a smallish man, with a ring of frizzy hair crowning a large dome, which was attached to a reedy frame. He looked as if he'd been carrying the weight of the world on his narrow shoulders for far too many years, and the slightly bewildered look in his eyes confirmed this view. When we walked in, he plastered a thin-lipped but pleasant smile on his careworn face, and greeted us with the kind of professional warmth and friendliness your small shopkeeper learns to master over a long and checkered career.

"Hello there," he said the moment he recognized our human, and there was a slight diminution of warmth as he eyed her expectantly. Instinctively the man knew that Odelia hadn't come to the shop to sample his wares, or spend lavishly on a gem, and his next words confirmed this. "You're here for that diamond, I presume? Has your uncle found the owner yet?" A flicker of hope shone in his pale blue eyes , but when Odelia shook her head, the flicker was replaced by a look of annoyance. "I was really hoping to get quick service from our local police department, Miss Poole."

"Mrs. Poole," I corrected the man from my position on the floor. Not that he seemed to notice. He directed a disinterested glance in my direction, then up at Odelia again.

"I don't feel entirely safe keeping that precious stone in my shop, you know. It's been one person after another who wants to take a look at it. The sooner you find the owner the better."

"Maybe you should close up the shop for now?" Odelia suggested, her voice laced with concern. That's my human for you: always concerned with the wellbeing of her fellow man, even when that fellow man doesn't show her the courtesy to remember that she's recently plighted her troth to another fellow man, and is now Mrs. Poole and no longer Miss Poole. Though of course one could argue that she's actually Mrs. Kingsley, but then Odelia had grown attached to the name her parents christened her with—she has, after all, been carrying that name for the past twenty-four years. One would get attached to something in less time, wouldn't you agree?

"Close my shop? I can't close my shop. I have a living to make, you know." He sighed as he drew a hand across his brow. "Though if that stone really is the famous Pink Lady, maybe I should close my doors for now. And upgrade my security system. I'm really not equipped to deal with the kind of attention a stone of that notoriety will no doubt garner."

"Do you think it's the actual Pink Lady?"

Mr. Linoski wavered. "It certainly looks like the genuine article. It has all the hallmarks—it even has very faint markings where you can see it was set."

"Set in a ring, you mean?"

The jeweler nodded. "Do you want to take a look?"

Odelia's face lit up with excitement. "Oh, can I?"

"Only because it's you," said Thormond, who looked old enough to have dandled Odelia on his knee when she was little. He disappeared through a small door, only to return promptly, carrying a small red velvet box in his hands. He was holding it reverently, as one would hold the hand of the Queen, when granted the rare privilege of an audience with that formidable lady. "Here she is," he said in hushed tones, betraying his reverence. He placed the box on the glass counter and opened it. Odelia bent over the item, and from her quick intake of breath I imagined this Pink Lady was a real sight to behold.

Odelia gestured to me and Dooley and asked, "Can I…"

The jeweler's face took on a stern expression, not unlike the wandmaker in the Harry Potter stories if a pimple-faced wizard had wandered into his store and declared that he didn't like the wand he bought and could he exchange it for one with more bells and whistles.

"I don't know…" said the jeweler hesitantly as Odelia first picked up Dooley, then me, and ever so carefully placed us on top of the glass counter.

It was a very nice glass counter, as glass counters go, and filled with the kind of stuff that makes people's heads spin: rings and bracelets and earrings and the like. It all glittered invitingly, and I could see why Mr. Linoski would be reluctant to allow two cats to prance around there: the counter's main purpose was to display the jeweler's wares, not as a runway for two cats to strut their stuff, especially since one of those cats was on the heavy side.

But then I caught sight of the Pink Lady—if indeed it was that fabled gem—and I stopped worrying about Thormond Linoski. The diamond was indeed a sight to behold. It was small and shiny and sparkly and, most assuredly, very pink!

"It's gorgeous, Max," said Dooley next to me. "But it's very small, isn't it?"

"It is very small," I said. "Although for a diamond I think it's plenty big."

"How much do you think it's worth?"

Odelia smiled and voiced that same question to the jeweler now. Thormond pursed his thin lips and glanced up at the ceiling, as if hoping to draw inspiration from the bright lights that shone down on the counter, and made his gem collection sparkle like a Christmas tree. "Well," he said after long and careful deliberation, "a diamond of this superb clarity, 24.78 carat in weight, pink coloring, cut to perfection by an expert cutter, would normally fetch seven figures at least."

"Seven figures?" asked Dooley, who'd been listening with rapt attention.

"Millions," said Odelia.

The jeweler nodded. "But if it is the Pink Lady, you have to add the history, and if my research is correct that would make this diamond, well, priceless."

"Priceless?" asked Odelia, as she glanced down at the gem, her eyes sparkling almost as fervently as the diamond itself.

"Priceless," said Thormond Linoski.

"I don't understand, Max," said Dooley. "How can a diamond have no price?"

"He means it's so expensive it's impossible to put a price on it," I explained.

"So… is it worth a lot, or nothing at all?" asked my friend, still confused.

"It's worth a lot," I said. "A whole lot."

"If you *had* to put a price on it," said Odelia. "How much…"

The jeweler shrugged helplessly. "Depends on the buyer. Stones like this are put up for auction, not sold in jewelry stores. We're talking many, many millions. Though, of course," he was quick to add, "the point of pricing is moot, since the stone will return to its rightful owner, and won't enter the market at any point."

"If it is the Pink Lady…"

The jeweler smiled now—a rare sight, and it caused his leathery face to stretch at the seams. "There's every chance that it is. But how it ended up on that beach? Now that is a complete mystery."

"And to think it might have stayed on that beach, and probably would have been swept away by the waves."

A look of constipation came over the scrawny gem specialist. "I'd rather prefer not to think about that. Imagine a precious and priceless gem like this, perfect in every respect, to be lost forever." He closed his eyes and shook his head. "It doesn't bear thinking. It simply doesn't."

"How do you think it ended up on the beach?"

"I can only imagine that whoever was in possession of the stone over the past thirty-odd years must have lost it somehow."

"The thief, you think?"

"Most assuredly. Are you familiar with the history of the Pink Lady?"

"Only what I've read on Wikipedia."

An expression of distaste flashed across the man's face, as if to convey the notion that your serious gem dealer doesn't consider Wikipedia a valuable source of information. "Well, the stone of course belonged to Sheikh Bab El Ehr, ruler of Khemed."

"Who gave it as a gift to his wife, didn't he?"

"Yes, he did," said Mr. Linoski with an indulgent smile. Even Wikipedia gets it right sometimes, that smile seemed to say. "The original stone was found in the Democratic Republic of Congo in 1967. At the time it was the largest stone ever retrieved in that particular mine. It was cut by an expert cutter in Antwerp, Belgium, heart of the international diamond industry, where the most renowned cutters are located, and then transferred to Khemed to become part of that country's collection of royal jewels. In 1985 it was set in an engagement ring and offered to the Sheikh's ninety-ninth wife, the lovely Laura Burns, who was only nineteen at the time of her wedding. She was, according to local lore, supposed to be the Sheikh's final wife, as he'd decided to stop short of reaching a full hundred, and he was rumored to be so enamored with the young lady that he wanted to gift her the most precious and expensive diamond in the world, the only thing that could possibly compete with his bride's radiant beauty. She wore the ring at their lavish wedding, and it's at that point that the story gets a little sketchy. The Sheikh's wife died at the one-year anniversary of her wedding, and the Pink Lady seems to have vanished without a trace after that."

"Poor Sheikh," said Odelia with feeling. "Losing his beloved wife like that must have been a terrible blow."

"At least he had his ninety-eight other wives to console him," Dooley pointed out.

"Did they ever find out what happened to the ring?" asked Odelia.

"No, like I said, things are a little sketchy, and no one seems to know what happened to the diamond after the Sheikh's wife died. But if you look closely at the stone, you can see very faint markings, where the stone was set in a ring." He offered Odelia his loupe to support his discovery.

She looked through the magnifying glass and said, "I see it. It's very faint, but those markings are definitely there."

"Which is why I'm almost certain that this is the fabled Pink Lady," said the jeweler with a smile of satisfaction. "Which of course will have to be confirmed."

"Who's going to have to confirm it?" asked Odelia as she put down the loupe.

"The insurance company contracted to insure the original ring would be my best bet," said Mr. Linoski. "Which is why your uncle needs to get in touch with the owners of this diamond as soon as possible—Sheikh Bab El Ehr's heirs. I believe that would be his son, who took over when his father died. Sheikh Bab El Ghat." He gave Odelia a look of concern. "I really don't feel safe keeping the stone here any longer than strictly necessary, you know."

"Maybe you should talk to my uncle," Odelia suggested as she put me and Dooley down on the floor again. "He might be able to arrange for an officer to keep an eye on your store."

The jeweler's face took on a look of annoyance. "I asked him that exact thing. And do you know what he said? That he couldn't spare anyone at the moment, and that it was up to me to make sure the stone was appropriately secured." He shook his grizzly head. "I ask you—is that what I pay taxes for?"

"Let me talk to my uncle. I'm sure I can convince him to post a couple of officers outside your shop."

A look of hope lit up the man's aged features. "Oh, I'd be most grateful. Most, most grateful."

"No problem." She offered the man a radiant smile. "We wouldn't want Hampton Cove to become known as the town where the famous Pink Lady went missing a second time, now would we?"

4

While Odelia went in search of her uncle to argue with the man about providing some much-needed security for the jeweler, Dooley and I decided to head on over to the hair salon and see what all the fuss was about with this flat earth business. After all, I was pretty sure that Dooley had exaggerated and that everything was just fine and dandy with Hampton Cove's go-to hair wizard.

But the moment we stepped into the shop, I immediately noticed that something was indeed off: there were no customers, which is exceptional, since Fido's business is usually buzzing with activity from morning till sometimes late at night, especially on the days that count like the holidays, when everyone wants to look just so.

Buster was seated on the windowsill, glancing up at his master with a forlorn look in his eyes, while said master was glancing through the window of his shop, a forlorn look in his eyes. He was dressed in his usual outfit: a white apron providing ample pockets where he tucked away the tools of his trade, such as there are combs and scissors and the like, only now his scissors weren't snipping away merrily as they usually did, and his many combs were as idle as his blow-dryer, clearly wondering why this sudden lull in a life that had always been busy as the proverbial bee.

When we entered, Fido looked up, an expectant gleam on his noble visage, but when he saw that it was just us, his face assumed its sad look again, and he resumed his idle gazing out of the window.

"Buster," I said, "what's going on?"

"Oh, hey, Max, Dooley," said the Maine Coon. "Well, as you can see there's something seriously wrong in the world of hair."

"Has this got something to do with the whole…"

"Flat Earth Society thing? Yeah, I think so. Fido has been going around trying to recruit new members, and this is what happened: people are staying away and going someplace else."

"But where are they going? Fido is the best hairdresser there is."

"My best bet would be the mall," said Buster. "One of those places where they whack off your hair for a couple of bucks. Clearly anything is better than to have to listen to Fido's ramblings."

"But… does he really believe all that stuff?" I asked, glancing up at the hirsute maestro, now temporarily out of work.

"Oh, yeah. In fact he's just accepted a position as the head of LIFES, the Long Island Flat Earth Society. His mission, should he choose to accept it, and of course he has, the doofus, is to build a vibrant community of flat earthlings and make Hampton Cove their Long Island headquarters."

"We have to do something, Max," said Dooley. "If this keeps up Fido will go out of business, and Buster will be homeless."

"I don't think it'll come to that," I assured my friend. And

Buster, too, of course, for the latter looked more than a little worried now that his human had gone off the deep end.

"We have to convince Fido that the earth is round," said Buster. "But how?"

"Well, just like Max suggested," said Dooley. "We need to take him on a trip around the world, and then when he discovers that he didn't fall off, but that he simply returned here, he'll know that this flat earth stuff is stuff and nonsense."

"We can't simply take the man on a trip around the world, Dooley," I said, once again engaging in a discussion I frankly never thought I'd have to get into—twice! "Like I already explained to you, it's going to take months, and we don't have the time." Or the money. I don't think traveling the world comes cheap nowadays, what with inflation and everything. Christopher Columbus had Ferdinand and Isabella to sponsor his expeditions, but who was going to hand us coffers full of Spanish gold? "Look, all we need to do is to ask Odelia or Marge or even Gran to reason with the man. I mean, how hard can it be to talk some sense into him?"

A man had wandered into the shop, rubbing his head, and clearly in the market for a haircut. "Wow, this is a first," he said as he glanced around at the empty chairs. "Can I…" He gestured to the chair Fido reserves for the customers ready to be divested of their surplus of hair.

"Please," said Fido, perking up now that he was once again requested to ply his trade. With a flourish he tied a barber cloth in front of his customer, tucked a protective strip along the man's neckline and, smiling a pleasant smile, said, "Have you ever wondered, Gerald, about the possibility that we've all been fed a bunch of lies since time immemorial?"

"Oh, sure," said Gerald, shifting a little in his chair and

making himself comfortable. "All you need to do is turn on the television and watch a couple of those political debates."

"I'm actually referring to the fact that the earth is flat, Gerald, not round the way we've always been told."

Gerald frowned. This clearly wasn't the direction he thought the conversation would go. "Flat?" he asked. "What are you talking about?"

"The planet is flat, Gerald," said Fido, not wasting time coming to the point. "Flat as a pancake."

"Huh. Is that a fact?"

"It is! Only you didn't know that, did you?"

"I sure didn't," said Gerald, directing a bewildered look at the hair master who was patting his client's head in that preparatory ritual favored by hairdressers the world over.

"I'll give you a flyer," said Fido confidentially, as he picked up a flyer from a stack he had lying next to the sink and the hair products he liked to apply. He handed the piece of paper to Gerald. "Everything you need to know is right there," he whispered conspiratorially.

"Um…" said Gerald as he helplessly glanced at the flyer, then stole a quick look at the door.

"Read it and weep," said Fido. "And then join us tonight at the meeting."

"The meeting?"

"I'm organizing the first-ever meeting of the Long Island branch of the Flat Earth Society. I'm the president," he added proudly as he took out his pair of scissors and snipped the air a couple of times for good measure. "Now how do you want your hair done, Gerald? The usual?"

But Gerald, whose face had adopted a pinched look, suddenly rose from the chair, ripped off the barber cloth and collar, and said, "I—I totally forgot but I—I have someplace I need to be. Right now!" And then he was hurrying for the door.

"Gerald?" asked Fido as he stood there, frozen. "Gerald, where are you going?"

"I'm sorry, Fido! Gotta run!"

"You forgot your flyer!" Fido yelled after the man. But Gerald was gone, his excess hair flapping in the breeze.

Buster turned to me. "See? This is what's been happening, Max. People come in, get a whiff of Fido's new project, and run out as quick as their legs can carry them."

"I see," I said, and I did. This was indeed a lot more serious than I'd thought at first.

"If this keeps up I will be out on the street," said our friend. "And Fido will be out on the street alongside me. We'll be living in a cardboard box in an alley and digging through dumpsters."

Fido, who'd sagged down on his chair again with a deep sigh, held up his scissors for a moment, then murmured, "Life is tough right now, sweetheart, but we're not giving up —oh, no. People have a right to know the truth."

"And now he's talking to his scissors," said Buster, shaking his head in dismay.

Clearly he was right: this called for an intervention. But what could we do? How could we drive this crazy idea from that poor man's head? Frankly I didn't have a clue. Like I said before, I'm not a shrink, so I don't know how to remedy what must surely be some kind of fatal flaw in the mental makeup of the human species. But I couldn't allow our friend to be kicked out of his own home because his human had gone cuckoo, so I placed a paw on Buster's shoulder and said solemnly, "We'll fix this, buddy. I promise."

"Why, thanks, Max," said Buster, perking up considerably. "I feel better already."

"So we're going on a trip around the world?" asked Dooley.

"No, Dooley," I said. "We're definitely not going on a trip around the world."

"Then what are we going to do?"

"I'll think of something."

"But what?"

Well now that, of course, was the big question.

5

Vesta Muffin was seated in the outside dining area of the Star hotel, her usual hangout of a morning, taking in the human traffic on Main Street, as was her habit. Her eagle-eyed glances would have discomforted the objects of her inspection, if they'd known they were under observation. In spite of her advanced age, there was nothing wrong with Vesta's eyesight, or her mind, which was as sharp as it had ever been—almost as sharp as her tongue, some of her detractors would have said.

Next to her, her friend Scarlett Canyon sat enjoying her iced caramel macchiato with extra foam and chocolate sprinkles on top. She licked her lips and said, "Did you hear about Fido?"

"Is he dead?" asked Vesta, perhaps with a touch too much eagerness in her voice.

Lately exactly nothing had happened in her world, and frankly she was bored, and eager for anything to happen, even the death of a fine hairdresser like Fido.

"He's joined a cult," said Scarlett, looking as pleased as the cat that got the cream that there was gossip she was aware of that her friend wasn't.

"A cult? What cult?"

"Here. He gave me this when I went in to have my roots done last night." She placed a flyer on the table and Vesta gratefully took it and gave it a quick perusal.

"Flat Earth Society? What in God's name is the Flat Earth Society?"

"Exactly what it says: they believe that the earth is flat and anyone who says different is an idiot."

"Huh," said Vesta, a small smile playing about her lips. "And Fido believes this crap?"

"He sure does. He talked me through the whole thing last night. I would have left, but he'd already applied the dye." She licked her lips again, only this time not for the purpose of sampling an extra helping of cream but reliving the scene. "He told me that I wouldn't believe the number of people who fall off the face of the earth each year, and it's all being hushed up by the government."

"Is that a fact?"

"He says that most deaths are actually attributed to people falling off the earth, and if only they'd tell people to watch out, a lot of casualties could be avoided. Birds, too."

"Birds?" asked Vesta, looking up from the flyer to take in her friend. Scarlett was dressed in a revealing red top of some kind of stretchy material, which hugged her impressive assets, and a miniskirt which accentuated her long legs. She might be Vesta's age, but she looked one or two decades younger. That bright red hair had a lot to do with it, of course. And Botox—plenty of Botox.

"Yeah, he says that a lot of birds go missing each year, because they fly past the point of no return, and then they can't find their way back."

"Poor birds."

"So of course I asked him what's beyond the earth, you know, if it makes birds get lost, and he says that the government knows, but they're refusing to tell us. Afraid to cause a panic." She nodded seriously as she took another sip from her delicious drink, then picked up one of the miniature cakes the Star hotel likes to provide its loyal customers.

"So what's so terrible that it might cause a panic?" asked Vesta, putting down the flyer and picking up her own drink, a nice big hot cocoa with plenty of cream on top and even a cherry this time, bless the server's heart.

"Fido says it must be something really, really terrible. Like monsters or something. And he says that armed guards make sure the monsters don't come and eat us all."

"So if there's armed guards, then why are people still falling over the edge?"

"It's a big world, Vesta. They probably don't have enough guards."

"So monsters, huh?"

"Yep." Scarlett was grinning now, obviously enjoying her tale. "One day a long time ago they came crawling out of the deep and ate all of the dinosaurs."

"They ate the dinosaurs? Those must be some big-ass monsters."

"Uh-huh. So that story about the dinosaurs going extinct after a meteor hit is all baloney—at least according to Fido."

"No meteor but monsters," said Vesta, nodding. "Gotcha."

"So when I was finally done, he gave me this flyer, and invited me to join his cult. He says the more people join up, the more pressure they can bring to bear on the world leadership to reveal the truth."

"About the people falling over the edge and the birds getting lost and the dinosaur-eating monsters."

"I told him I'd think about it."

"You know what we should do?" said Vesta as she yawned

and stretched. "We should go to this meeting." She was tapping the flyer.

Scarlett stared at her. "What are you talking about?"

"Scarlett, I don't know about you, but I'm bored. Nothing ever happens in this town, and if this keeps up I'm going to die of boredom. You do know that people can die from boredom, right? You see it happen all the time with the folks that retire. Three months later they're dead. Worked all their lives, forty years on the job, and three months into their retirement, bam, they drop dead."

"You're not retired, though. You still work at the doctor's office."

"Yeah, but that's a borefest, too. I want some excitement, honey. Something to keep my mind engaged. And this flat earth business is just the ticket. I can feel it in my bones."

"I don't know, Vesta. It looks a little crazy to me."

"Of course it looks crazy. Because it is crazy. So why don't you and I infiltrate this organization and find out what's going on?"

"Oh, I know what's going on. A bunch of crazies getting together and driving each other even crazier than they already are. What surprises me, though, is how a guy like Fido would get involved in a thing like that. He never struck me as a nutter."

"That's what we need to find out. If these people can snag Fido, who's next? Pretty soon this whole town will be part of this cult, and then when the FBI comes knocking, we'll be the ones to save the day. We'll be like Deep Throat."

"What throat?"

"Never mind what throat. Let's do this."

"If you say so," said Scarlett, dubiously.

6

Marge Poole was reading a book and was so engrossed by the exciting tale the author had spun that she didn't even notice a customer had entered the library and was standing in front of her desk. Only when the person cleared her throat did she finally look up.

"Oh, hey, Mrs. Samson," she said. Margaret Samson was one of her regulars, and came in every week, sometimes even twice a week, to load up on reading material. Her genre of choice was steamy romance, which for a lady as aged as she was sometimes came as a surprise to those who saw her fill her little basket with her favorite books. "I have that book you asked me to look out for," Marge said as she put down her own book and picked up a tome she'd put aside for Mrs. Samson. It was called Fierce Hunk, by Courtney Divine, and featured a picture of a young man with an impressive six-pack and a sort of smoldering look in his eyes.

Mrs. Samson's own eyes lit up. "Oh, goodie," she said. "I've been waiting for that one. I do wish these writers would write faster, Marge. Can't you tell them to write faster? It's been months since Fierce Heart came out, and I just know I'll have to wait months for Fierce Betrayal, the third book in the trilogy."

"I'd tell her if I knew her," said Marge with an indulgent smile as she placed the book aside. From experience she knew that the old lady would load up on more reading material. One book was only going to keep her occupied for a couple of hours. She read a book a day, and sometimes even that wasn't enough. "You could always write to her," she suggested.

"Write Courtney Divine?" asked Mrs. Samson, raising her eyebrows in surprise. "You mean like a letter?"

"No, an email. Or you could even find her on social media, and get in touch with her that way."

"I don't know about that," said Mrs. Samson dubiously. "She probably doesn't want to be bothered."

"I'm sure she'd love to hear from such a loyal fan as yourself. Here, I'll write down her email and you can go over to one of the internet computers and write to her." She handed the old lady a piece of paper with the email.

Mrs. Samson stared at it curiously and with a touch of reverence. "But... what do I tell her?"

"Just tell her how much you love her books, and tell her you can't wait for the next one to come out."

"Okay," said the old romance addict. "I guess I can do that."

Marge watched her trot off in the direction of the bank of internet computers, and smiled. An avid reader herself, she could absolutely relate to Mrs. Samson, who considered the characters in the books she read almost as real as the people in her own life.

She picked up the book she'd been reading and was soon engrossed in the story. It was about a woman of humble descent who met a sheikh and fell in love. Part one depicted their whirlwind romance, and he'd just proposed to her and she'd accepted and was rushing home to tell her mom and dad all about it and also to show them the diamond ring the sheikh had gifted her, containing a very precious and unique diamond called the Pink Lady.

Just then, her phone chimed, and when she glanced over, she saw her daughter was trying to reach her. "Hey, honey," she said. "I'm just reading the most amazing book. The Sheikh's Passion. Have you read it?"

"No, Mom," said Odelia. "I'm with Uncle Alec right now, and we need your help."

"My help?"

"Wait—I'll hand the phone to him."

There was a rustling sound, and then her brother Alec's voice sounded in her ear. "Marge, I need to ask you a big, big favor."

"Sure," she said. "Though if it's about tonight's menu, it's fish. I already took it out of the freezer, and if we don't eat it tonight it's going to spoil."

"It's not about the fish. It's about a diamond." He cleared his throat. "Have you ever heard about a diamond called the Pink Lady?"

Marge blinked, then her eyes slowly traveled to the cover of the book on her desk. It depicted a very large and very pink diamond. "The Pink Lady?"

"Yeah. It was a diamond that went missing thirty years ago. It used to belong to a sheikh's wife—anyway, long story short, it disappeared, and now it's turned up again. On the beach."

"Amazing," she breathed, as she turned the book over and perused the back cover, where a picture of the author had been printed. It was a woman with thick curly blond hair, looking confidently into the camera. Her name was Loretta Gray, and The Sheikh's Passion was her debut novel.

"So the people that found the diamond took it to Thormond Linoski, the jeweler on Carmel Street, and now he's afraid for his safety, and the safety of the diamond. And as long as we don't know for sure who it belongs to, I was thinking that maybe we should keep it in a place no one would ever think to look."

"And where is that?"

"You have a small safe in your bedroom, right?"

"Uh-huh."

"Well, why don't we put the stone there until we can figure out what to do with it?"

"Why don't you keep it at the police station? Don't you think it'll be safer there?"

"This was actually your daughter's idea," said the Chief. "Wait, here she is."

"Mom?" said Odelia. "So Mr. Linoski has asked for extra security, but Uncle Alec can't spare anyone right now, and so we were thinking that the best way would be for the diamond to be kept in a secret place."

"So why not the police station?" she repeated.

"Wait, I'll hand over Uncle Alec again."

"Marge, the police station is the first place thieves will look when they find out about that stone. And trust me, they will find out, since the parents of the little girl who found the stone have already been blabbing about it to anyone who would listen. It's all over the news—they even gave an interview to WLBC-9 and everything."

"Okay, sure, if you think this is a good idea."

"It wasn't my idea," said Alec. "I wanted to put it in the police station lockup but Odelia—wait, I'm passing the phone to her."

"Mom, I think we can't afford for this stone to go missing again. The last time it took thirty years for it to turn up, and also, we don't know how it ended up on that beach. Maybe the people who took it lost it and are now looking for it. And also," she lowered her voice, "I'm not sure we can trust the people here."

"Here? You mean at the precinct?"

"Well, there's been an incident."

"What incident?"

"I interviewed Mr. Linoski, and five minutes after I left two cops showed up and told him Uncle Alec had asked them to come and pick up the diamond. Only Mr. Linoski had a bad feeling, and told them the diamond had already been picked up and wasn't at the shop anymore."

"Oh, dear."

"Marge, Alec again," said her brother. "Look, I'm still looking into this—maybe it was some kind of misunderstanding, I don't know. But for now let's just play it safe and keep that stone where only we know where to find it, all right?"

"If you think that's best."

"What's the combination of the safe?"

"Oh, I have absolutely no idea. You'll have to ask Tex."

"Mom?" said Odelia, taking the phone from her uncle again. "I'm going to pick up the diamond, and I'm taking it to your place, okay? And if anyone asks? We never had this conversation, and you've never heard of the Pink Lady."

"If you say so, honey," said Marge, still feeling a little dazed by the coincidence. And as she placed down the phone and picked up her book again, she continued reading with even more fervor than before.

7

We met up with Odelia while she was setting a course for the jeweler once more, and of course we quickly decided to hook our little wagon to her locomotive and see what she was up to.

"Odelia, we need to talk," said Dooley, adopting a serious tone.

"Not now, Dooley," said Odelia as she took large strides in the direction of Gems World, and when we looked up I think we both noticed she was looking exceptionally serious.

"What's going on?" I asked therefore. Our human is not one of those happy-go-lucky people, but neither is she a person who goes through life with a large chip on her shoulder, or even prone to the kind of moodiness and gloominess some of your more famous detectives seem to suffer from. Take your Sam Spade, for instance, or even your Philip Marlowe. Not exactly a pair of chuckle buddies. No, they're tough fellas, sucking from cigarettes and talking through the side of their mouths and never happier than when giving some heavy a knuckle sandwich.

"I'm sorry, you guys," said Odelia, lowering her voice as her eyes flitted to and fro. "Best if we don't talk right now." She then whispered, "We're taking the diamond to a safe place!"

"Gotcha!" I whispered back, and allowed my own eyes to follow the same stroboscopic pattern set by my human. If the walls have ears, the same goes for streets. There's always someone about with an unhealthy interest in a woman talking to her cats, and ready to take photographic or even videographic evidence of same. Ever since the advent of the smartphone, privacy seems to have become a thing of the past, and before you know it your every single move is documented on some Facebook page and shared by a bunch of strangers.

"Mum's the word," I said, and mimicked zipping up my lips to give a good example.

"Why is mum the word, Max?" asked Dooley. "I mean, I know mum is *a* word, but why is it *the* word?"

"It's an expression, Dooley," I explained. "It means it's time to keep quiet."

This time it was Dooley's turn to glance around as if expecting a contingent of scary men in trench coats and masks to get ready to bodily drag us into an unmarked van.

"It's just that this is a very delicate operation, Dooley," I explained. "We're moving the Pink Lady to a safe place, and so it's very important not to draw any unwanted attention to ourselves. You never know who might be watching."

And in fact now that I thought of it, this wasn't such a far-fetched idea either. If the people who had stolen that stone thirty years ago, and had now lost it on the beach, had gotten wind that the stone was to be found at Gems World, they might have posted a lookout in front of the jeweler while thinking up ways and means of getting their hands on that precious diamond once more.

Odelia stepped into the store, after glancing left and right for good measure, and we followed in her wake.

"Oh, hi, Mrs. Poole," said Mr. Linoski, looking pleased as punch to see us again—or at least the human element in our small band of three. "I've got the stone ready for you." He proceeded to slide an envelope across the counter, making certain not to glance down at it, and in doing so acting very conspicuously indeed.

"Why is he acting so weird, Max?" asked Dooley. "They're all acting so weird, him and Odelia both."

"You never know who's watching, Dooley," I said. "And right now maybe the bad people are watching the store. For all we know they could even have set up shop in an apartment across the street, watching us through their binoculars, to find out what's going on."

Cleverly enough Odelia kept herself in front of the counter, and effectively obscured that envelope from view of whoever might be watching in my hypothetical scenario. In fact she was making as little movement as possible while she surreptitiously slipped the envelope into her purse and, like the jeweler, didn't even bother to look down.

Very smooth!

"What can you tell me about the two cops that were in here?" she asked now.

"Here, I have them on video," said the jeweler helpfully. He looked very much relieved, and I didn't wonder. If I was keeping a diamond worth millions in my store, I'd be relieved too if someone took it off my hands.

The jeweler now showed Odelia his phone, and she frowned as she watched the footage. "Well, I'll be damned," she muttered.

"Do you recognize them?" asked Mr. Linoski curiously.

Odelia nodded thoughtfully.

"So are they police officers? Should I have handed them

the diamond? Only I didn't feel safe doing that, you see. Especially after your uncle told me that he didn't have anyone to spare who could guard my store. And then suddenly these two officers showed up—"

"It's all right," said Odelia, giving the man a reassuring smile. "I know who they are. And you absolutely did the right thing, Mr. Linoski."

"Oh, that's a great relief. You see, I felt bad not complying with a direct order from the strong arm of the law, and I was actually on the verge of handing over the diamond. I've always prided myself in being a law-abiding citizen, and so when they asked me to hand over the stone I immediately assumed—"

"It's fine," said Odelia, stemming the flow of words. "I think I better be going now, and make sure this little gem is tucked away safely where no one will find it." She patted her purse, and it was clear that she wanted to get out of there as soon as possible and get this most dangerous assignment over with posthaste.

"Thank you so much, Mrs. Poole," said the jeweler, and clasped his hands together gratefully. "Your uncle told me this was your idea, and I want you to know that I can't thank you enough."

"That's all right. You did your part, Mr. Linoski, and for that I'm sure the owners of the Pink Lady will be most grateful."

The jeweler licked his lips. "Will there be a finder's fee, you think? I know I didn't technically find the stone, but I was instrumental in its safekeeping, so I just wondered…"

"As soon as we can track down the owners, I'll be sure to tell them what an important part you played," Odelia assured the man. She was slowly backtracking to the door, eager to get on her way.

We followed suit, and soon we were out on the sidewalk

again, and lo and behold: a car had driven up, and we recognized the person behind the wheel as Odelia's husband Chase.

"Get in," he said, and we all did. "And now let's get the hell out of here," he grunted, and was soon peeling away from the curb and making good time for the good ol' homestead.

8

If Odelia and Chase had stuck around for just a little while longer, they would have discovered that all of their precautions hadn't been in vain. For the moment they were out of sight, two men appeared in the window above the bakery across the street from Thormond Linoski's gem emporium. One of the men was heavyset and suffered the misfortune of having to go through life without the benefit of a neck, while his partner in crime was a small, scrawny type with the face of a ferret.

"Dammit," said the ferrety one, whose name was Jerry Vale, and had been in and out of jail so many times the episodes had blurred in his mind. "I knew we should have grabbed that thing when we had the chance."

"But how, Jer?" asked the no-neck one, who answered to the name Johnny Carew. "How could we grab the thing?"

"Simple. You could have knocked that guy's block off, and then we could have grabbed the stone."

"But you said he probably kept it in the vault."

"Then you could have told him to take it out of the vault, or else."

"Or else what, Jer? You said no violence. And besides, we're on the straight and narrow now, and people on the straight and narrow don't go and knock other people's blocks off."

"Mh," said Jer, who looked as if he hadn't exactly figured this one out himself yet.

"Besides, now we know that Odelia has it, things are a lot simpler."

"Simpler?" Jerry whipped his head around to look at his associate so fast it cricked—he did have a neck, and right now it hurt from having sat there in their small apartment, keeping an eye on the comings and goings across the street. "Simpler? It's just become a lot more complicated!"

"But don't you see, Jer?" said his friend, holding up two hands the size of coal shovels. "Now we can simply walk up to Odelia and tell her nicely to hand over the stone. Easy peasy!"

"Nothing doing," Jerry grunted irritably. He rubbed his painful neck. It was bad enough that they'd lost the damn stone, but they were forced to stay in an apartment the size of a broom closet, and sleep on a mattress that was so worn out his back was killing him. "I know Odelia Poole, Johnny. The moment she got hold of that rock she's never letting go again. No, we can kiss that precious Pink Lady goodbye. It's gone. And you and me missed the chance of a lifetime."

"Don't be so glum, Jer," said his friend, placing one of those coal shovels on Jerry's shoulder and squeezing. "You know what we should do? We should talk to Marge. Marge likes us. In fact she likes us so much there's nothing she wouldn't do for us."

"Says you."

"No, but it's true. Remember how nice she was when she offered us that job at the library?"

"Mh."

"I say we go over there right now and have a nice chat with her. We'll simply explain the situation and I'm sure she'll do the right thing."

"Mh."

If Jerry didn't sound convinced, it was because he had a much more dour outlook on life than Johnny, who was one of those rare people who always saw the good in others, unlike Jerry, who always saw the worst.

"My neck hurts," he lamented, "and so does my back. I'm going to the pharmacy." He then wagged a finger in his friend's face. "You stay here, you hear me? You've messed up once, I don't need you to mess up again."

"Sure, Jer," said Johnny as he allowed his large body to drop down on the crooked and aged old couch and flicked on the small TV set in the corner of the room. "Whatever you say."

🐾

*I*n spite of the fact that he'd promised his friend to stay put, Johnny soon felt a compelling need to break that promise and head out of the apartment he shared with his partner in crime—or uncrime, ever since they'd reformed. A large body like the one he carried through life needs to be fed at regular intervals, and this was what posed the problem. He'd been watching the adventures of the men and women on Passion Island, one of those reality shows that seemed to be all the rage, when he felt his stomach loudly protest. So he went in search of food. Only when he opened the cupboard, there was very little that would satisfy a big guy like him: apart from a stack of sardine cans and an empty bag of Wonder Bread, only empty space was to be found. The fridge was even worse: apart from the remnants of last night's pizza, which he ate, and two cold beers, which he drank, the thing was empty.

So Johnny decided there was only one thing to do: he needed to do some shopping. Jerry could thank him later. And he'd only just stepped out of the apartment when he came upon a handsome-looking man with a very snazzy coiffure, who pressed a flyer into his hands and said, "Read this, my friend. It will open your eyes." Since his eyes were already open, Johnny didn't know how to respond to this. The other man jumped into the breach by adding, "We've all been lied to, my friend. And it's time that we learned the truth."

"The truth?" asked Johnny. His mama had always taught him to speak the truth, so this proposition appealed to him greatly.

"Just read the information on the flyer," the man suggested. "It's all there. The truth, the whole truth and nothing but the truth."

These words were imminently familiar to Johnny, as he'd heard them being used in the many, many trials he'd participated in over the course of a long and industrious criminal career. The man reminded him of something, and for a moment he couldn't put his finger on it. But then finally he got it. "Are you a brother, brother?" he asked, his eyes lighting up. His weeks spent as a Jehovah's Witness were still fresh in his mind. It had been a period in his life fraught with frustration, but also with a keen sense of kinship with the other men and women who had gone door to door to spread the word of the Lord to the world, only to have the door thrown in their faces almost each and every time.

"Yes, I am, brother," said the man, placing a brotherly hand on Johnny's broad shoulder.

"I lost faith, brother," Johnny confessed. "I knocked on so many doors, and no one would answer. So I finally stopped knocking." Also there was the fact that he and Jerry had been arrested while out proselytizing. It hadn't gone down well with their congregation, unfortunately. He didn't think he should mention that minor detail to this man, in whom he now recognized a kindred spirit.

"Come to the meeting tonight, brother," said the man, as he held out a hand.

Johnny shook it warmly. Somehow he felt this was fate. When at his lowest ebb, along came this savior, and he, for one, was adamant to grab onto this life raft with both hands.

"What's your name, brother?" he asked finally.

"Fido Siniawski," said the other man.

"I'm Johnny," said Johnny. "Is it all right if I bring a friend?"

"Brother," said Fido, "you can bring all the friends you want. The more the merrier."

And so it was with a spring in his step that Johnny Carew headed to the General Store. A spring in his step and a small stack of flyers in his pocket, to hand out to anyone who would listen. Now all he needed was his trusty bible and a crisp white shirt and nice tie and he was back in business, baby!

9

We'd finally arrived home, the precious stone still safe in Odelia's purse and no carjackers or purse-snatchers or other scum of the earth having waylaid us or even having showed their ugly faces, and frankly I heaved a sigh of relief.

"Now I think I know what those money transporters must feel like," said Dooley, who had experienced the same unabated tension from the moment that diamond had been placed in our possession to the moment we finally arrived home. "It's very stressful, don't you think, Max?"

"Extremely stressful," I agreed.

"I saw a documentary on the Discovery Channel once and they said money transporters suffer more from stomach ulcers than the average person. I hope Odelia won't turn this into a regular thing." He grabbed his stomach. "I think I can feel an ulcer developing already, Max. Can't you?"

"I think I'm fine for now, Dooley," I said with a smile. "No ulcers anywhere in sight, I'm happy to say."

"I'm not so sure, Max," he said, giving me a dubious look. "It takes years for an ulcer to develop, so one could already be there, only you don't know it until it's too late. Same with cancer."

"I'm sure we're both fine, Dooley," I said as we entered the house in Odelia and Chase's wake. "It's just one little trip through town, not a lifetime of transporting precious cargo in an armored car."

"Still," he said as we set paw inside our living room and immediately relaxed. I don't know about you, but I always feel there's no place like home, is there?

"So what do you plan to do with it?" asked Chase as Odelia took the envelope the jeweler had handed her and opened it.

"I'd like to put it in Mom and Dad's safe immediately," said Odelia as she studied the stone. It didn't look all that remarkable to me, to be honest. In fact it looked just like a piece of pink glass. Why a tiny little stone like that should be worth millions was absolutely beyond me.

"So is there a picture of a pink lady in that stone, Odelia?" asked Dooley eagerly. "Can I see it?"

Odelia laughed, and when she translated Dooley's words for her husband, the burly cop emitted a hearty laugh, too. "The diamond might be called the Pink Lady, Dooley," he explained as he crouched down and gave my friend a tickle under his chin, "but there's no image of a pink lady inside it."

"There isn't?" said Dooley, looking distinctly disappointed. "But why?"

"Because there simply isn't," said Odelia as she tucked the diamond away again. "Let's get this over with, shall we? I'll feel safer once this stone is behind lock and key."

Together she and Chase walked out the back door and into the backyard, then disappeared through the opening in the hedge that separates our backyard from Odelia's parents' little patch of green heaven. And since our mission now seemed at an end, Dooley and I decided to take a breather and take up our position on the smooth lawn once more, before that fickle sun decided to call it a day and turned off the heat.

And we'd just been lying there for a couple of minutes when a voice intruded upon the peace and quiet.

"What's all this I'm hearing about a Pink Lady?" asked the voice.

I didn't even have to open my eyes to know who the voice belonged to: Harriet, our white Persian friend. She was trotting up to us, her tail pointing at the sky like a flagpole, Brutus in her wake.

"The Pink Lady isn't actually a real lady," said Dooley helpfully. "And she's not even an image of a pink lady. She's just a pink stone, so why they're calling her a lady I really don't know."

"Probably because the diamond is pink and was a gift for a lady," I said.

"So where is this diamond now?" asked Harriet as she lay herself down next to us.

"It's in Marge and Tex's safe," I said. "The jeweler didn't feel comfortable having it at the shop, and Uncle Alec didn't feel comfortable having it at the police station, so Odelia thought it would be a good idea to put it where nobody would think to look, at least until they can get in touch with the owners of the precious gem."

"Precious, huh?" said Brutus, joining us on the lawn. "How much, you think?"

"I'm not sure," I said. "The jeweler told us it's priceless, but he also said it's worth millions, so make of that what you will."

"Millions," said the butch black cat, and a strange glimmer came into his eyes, and when I glanced over to Harriet, I saw that the same glimmer was mirrored in her strikingly green eyes as well.

"It used to belong to the Sheikh's wife," Dooley explained. "She was the Sheikh's ninety-ninth wife, but then she died, and then the stone disappeared, and then the Sheik died, though I'm not sure when, but now his son is the new sheikh, and I'm not sure how many wives he's got, but then the stone turned up on the beach, and then fake cops tried to take the stone, and Odelia recognized the fake cops but she wouldn't tell us who they were, though she whispered their names to Chase in the car, and I think she said it was Johnny and Jerry. Isn't that right, Max?"

I nodded. Even though for some reason Odelia hadn't wanted us to find out that our two criminal friends were up to their old tricks again, of course we'd heard what she said loud and clear.

"So millions, huh?" said Brutus, as if he hadn't heard Dooley's entire iteration of the story. "That's a lot of dough, fellas. Imagine what we could do with millions."

"Odelia could buy herself and her family a castle," said Harriet, "and then we could live like kings." That glimmer was shining more brightly than ever now. "She could really pamper us and we could all live in the lap of luxury if the Pooles had those millions at their disposal."

"First off, they don't have millions at their disposal," I said, deciding the best way to deal with this glimmer, which I recognized as the glimmer of greed, was to nip it in the bud. "And second, there's nothing millions could buy that we don't already have. I mean, we have food, and a perfect home, and the best humans, and great friends—what difference are millions going to make?"

Harriet turned an icy glare on me. "God, Max, you're so pedestrian."

"Of course Max is a pedestrian," said Dooley. "He's never learned how to drive a car."

"Don't you see this is the chance of a lifetime?" Harriet

continued, ignoring Dooley. "If Odelia sells that stone to the highest bidder we're set for life. None of the Pooles will ever have to work again, they could spend the rest of their lives on a yacht in the South of France and live the most amazing wonderful fabulous life!"

"I don't think I'd like to live on a yacht," said Dooley, striking the discordant note. "I was on a cruise ship and I almost got eaten by a big nasty bird. So I guess I haven't found my sea paws yet."

"Oh, Dooley," said Harriet with a sigh. "You're almost as pedestrian as Max."

"More pedestrian," Brutus pointed out.

"I think I'll have a word with Odelia now," said Harriet as she eagerly glanced in the direction of the hedge. "It's obvious she needs a little guidance from her favorite feline."

So she and Brutus skedaddled, and Dooley and I were left staring after them.

"I didn't know Harriet was Odelia's favorite feline," said Dooley.

"She isn't," I assured him. "It's just that Harriet wants something from Odelia and she thinks flattery will get her there."

"Do you really think Odelia will sell the Pink Lady and become a millionaire?"

"No, I don't think so. She might even refuse a reward if one is offered. She'll insist that seeing the happiness on the rightful owner's face is enough reward for her."

"Well, phew. I really don't want to live on a yacht, Max."

"Me, neither, Dooley."

10

Now that the diamond was safe, and the powers that be were engaged in tracking down its rightful owner, it was time to tackle the problem that really should be at the forefront of our minds: how to save Buster's human from self-destruction!

And so as we lay there, I rallied my mental faculties and directed them toward solving that seemingly unsolvable problem.

"So how do you convince someone who's one hundred percent convinced of something that they're heading down a dangerous path?" I asked, thinking out loud as I sometimes do.

"I think we have to tell Harriet that money doesn't make you happy," said Dooley, misinterpreting my question. "And the only way to do that is by making her rich for a day."

"Rich for a day?" I asked. "What do you mean?"

"Haven't you ever seen that show where two families trade places? A rich family goes to live in the house of a poor family and the other way around. They swap lives for a while, to see how the other half lives. Brutus and Harriet could swap places with a pair of rich cats for a couple of weeks, and I'm sure they'll see that even rich cats have their problems, the same way we do."

"Mh," I said, thinking this over. "You know, there's something in that, Dooley."

"I know. It's a very popular show," said my friend. "Gran and I watch it all the time. It's very funny."

I didn't see how swapping lives would be funny, but then Gran has a very peculiar sense of humor.

"The only problem is: where do we find a pair of rich cats, and how do we make them want to swap places with Harriet and Brutus?"

"Actually I wasn't thinking of Harriet and Brutus," I said.

"You weren't?"

"No, I was thinking about Buster."

"Buster? I don't think Buster wants to be rich."

"No, but he doesn't want to go and live in the gutter either. So we need to make sure Fido steps back from the brink before it's too late. And what better way to do that than to confront him with the consequences of his actions? Only not at some distant point in the future, but right now." Dooley was staring at me. "I'm sorry," I said. "Don't mind me. I'm just spitballing."

"I get that all the time," he said, nodding. "Only I call it chucking up a hairball. Though it's been a while since I had one."

I smiled and then closed my eyes to give this matter a little more thought.

"Odelia?"

"Mh?"

"What are you going to do with that diamond?"

Odelia glanced down at Harriet. She was a little preoccupied right now, what with holding a million-dollar gem in the palm of her hand, and a gem with a long history at that. "What do you mean?" she asked as she deftly opened her mom and dad's safe and peered inside. It was one of those wall safes her parents had installed in the bedroom. Right now it only held a couple of Dad's Superman comics, which he bought years ago when he had the idea he wanted to be a comics collector. But since, as hobbies go that had been a costly one, he'd soon switched to collecting garden gnomes instead.

"Well, are you going to sell the diamond or what?"

"I can't sell a diamond that's not mine, Harriet," she said as she placed the envelope with the stone inside the safe, then closed the little door again, and gave the dial a couple of turns.

"But if you sell it, how much do you think you'll get for it?" Harriet insisted.

She frowned as she took in the question. "I just told you the stone isn't mine to sell. So what does it matter how much I would get for it?"

"I think you should sell it," Brutus piped up.

She glanced down at the twosome, and saw that they were both eyeing her a little feverishly.

"What are they saying?" asked Chase with a smile.

"They want me to sell the diamond," she said with a shrug.

"We can't sell it," Chase pointed out. "It doesn't belong to us."

"So what if you sell it back to the owners?" Harriet suggested. "How much do you think they'll pay? Millions? A billion?"

She now recognized the look in her cats' eyes. It was the same kind of look gold diggers get when they're on a riverbank sifting through the mud. Or the kind of feverish fervor some of those bitcoin miners experienced when the value of their bitcoin suddenly hit the roof.

"Look, the stone isn't mine to sell," she repeated. "And besides, you can't put a value on a stone like the Pink Lady. Its value is an emotional one. It was a gift from Sheikh Bab El Ehr to his wife, a symbol of their love. How do you put a price on something like that? You can't."

"So how about a finder's fee? How much do you think these people will pay for the privilege of getting their treasured diamond back?"

She took a seat next to Chase on the bedroom bench and regarded her cats sternly. "I have to confess I'm a little disappointed in you right now, Harriet. You, too, Brutus. For you even to suggest such a thing is just... I mean, really?"

Harriet looked surprised by this. "What do you mean?"

"We don't go around trying to make a fast buck, Harriet. That's not who we are. We try to do the right thing, not get rich off other people's misery."

Harriet had the decency to look embarrassed, and so did Brutus.

She rubbed the Persian's head. "Look, I know the notion of possessing a fabulously precious stone like the Pink Lady can make your head spin. But we can't let it affect us. There's more to life than money, you guys. We can't let this diamond change who we are: decent human beings... and cats," she added with a smile.

"I'm sorry," said Harriet, and Odelia noticed how that dangerous gleam had disappeared from her eyes. "I don't know what came over me. I just..." she shook her head, as if trying to rid herself of a pesky flea. "I'm sorry."

"It's all right," said Odelia. "I think you caught a bug, honey, and so did you, Brutus."

"A bug?" asked the pretty Persian, looking horrified. "What bug?"

"The diamond bug. And now scram, will you? Chase and I have some stuff to discuss."

She watched as Harriet and Brutus disappeared through the door, then closed it.

"So why didn't you want the cats to know about Johnny and Jerry gunning for that stone?" asked Chase.

"Because I don't want to get them involved any more than they already are. Petty crime is one thing, but this diamond…" She darted a glance at the portrait of a gnome, which Dad had hung in front of the safe, and which swung on a set of hinges to obscure its presence. "It scares me, you know. You saw what happened with Harriet and Brutus just now. Somehow the presence of the Pink Lady brings out the worst in people, and I don't want my cats to get hurt."

"They'll be fine," said Chase as he placed an arm around her shoulders. She leaned in and her husband's embrace felt good, as did the kiss he placed on her temple. "We'll find out who this gem belongs to, give it back to them, and that's it."

She sighed deeply. Somehow she had a feeling it wouldn't be quite so simple. She just hoped she was wrong.

11

Marge was frowning before herself as she locked up the library and started on her way home. She'd googled the author of the book she'd been reading but had unfortunately drawn a blank. It seemed as if there wasn't much of an internet presence for Loretta Gray, which was unusual in this day and age. The woman didn't even have a website, which was even more surprising, or even a Facebook page.

And she'd just reached the sidewalk and took a left to head in the direction of home and hearth, when suddenly the door of a car that stood parked at the curb opened and that very same Loretta Gray stepped out!

Marge immediately recognized the author from her author picture, in spite of the sunglasses the writer was wearing. Her blond hair shone like spun gold, and she was dressed in an expensive green suit, her feet clad in equally expensive high heels. All in all, she looked like a million bucks. Exactly like what Marge would have expected the authoress of The Sheikh's Passion to look.

"Marge Poole?" asked the woman as she took off her sunglasses.

"Yes?" said Marge, highly surprised by this sudden turn of events. "You're Loretta Gray, aren't you?"

The author smiled. "Have we met?"

"No, but I've just been reading… Wait, here it is." She reached into her canvas bag and took out the book. "I've been reading your book," she said, holding up her library copy.

The woman's smile vanished. "Oh," she said. "I see."

"I love it," said Marge. "I think it's an amazing story, and it so vividly describes what happened it's almost as if…"

"Yes," said the woman, glancing down at the book with a strange look in her eyes.

"Almost as if it's autobiographical," Marge finished, and the moment she spoke the words, she regretted them, for a hard look appeared on the woman's face.

"Look, I'm not here to discuss my book," she said, her voice clipped and her demeanor businesslike. "I saw on the news that the Pink Diamond was found on the beach yesterday, and I was hoping to talk to the person who found it."

"Oh, but that wasn't me," said Marge, wondering why an author would resent discussing her work. Then again, writers are a strange breed, of course. Maybe she'd once wrote it and now regretted it. Or it reminded her of a time in her life she'd rather forget.

"No, I know it wasn't you," said Miss Gray. "But I called the TV station and they said they couldn't divulge the identity of the finder—even though they interviewed her live on the air—and so I asked if I could speak to someone with knowledge of the situation, and they referred me to the Mayor. But when I called Town Hall, a secretary said the Mayor couldn't take my call, since she was busy, and referred me to the police station. And when I called there…"

"They foisted you off, too."

"So I asked the woman who answered my call if she could put me in touch with Olivia Wynn, the little girl who found the diamond, or if there was anyone in this town who would talk to me about what happened, and she gave me your name. She literally said, 'If there's anything you want to know about what goes on in Hampton Cove, you gotta talk to Marge Poole. She's the town librarian, and we all know what librarians are like: a bunch of nosy busybodies!'" She smiled. "I wouldn't have put it that way, but in a sense she does have a point, however crudely expressed. When I was little and I had a difficult school assignment or an essay to write, the librarian was always the first person my mom told me to go and see."

"And did it work?" asked Marge, happy that the initial awkwardness between them had dissipated.

"Sure. We had a very nice librarian in the town I grew up in. Her name was Hildegarde Procak, and she always had all the answers. Of course my questions were probably not that difficult, since I was only nine."

"Oh, but you would be surprised by how difficult kids' questions can be," Marge said with a laugh.

"So what can you tell me about the Pink Lady?" asked the authoress.

"I'm afraid I don't know all the details. Only that the diamond was found on the beach yesterday, quite by accident, by a little girl who was playing in the sand with her little brother—"

"Olivia Wynn."

"See? I didn't even know that. All I know is she gave it to her mom, who immediately realized this was not a piece of colored glass and took it to a jeweler in town to have it appraised."

"And the jeweler recognized it as a precious stone and

called the police," said the woman with a nod. "Any idea how a diamond like the Pink Lady ended up on a beach in the Hamptons?"

"No idea," said Marge truthfully. "But if I may ask: why are you so interested in this diamond? Is it connected with your book?" She held up her copy of The Sheikh's Passion. And watched as the author immediately stiffened again.

"No, nothing to do with the book," she said, almost snappishly, as if Marge had said the wrong thing. Then she abruptly turned on her heel and strode back to her car. But before she opened the door, she seemed to have a change of heart, and returned on her steps. "Do you… do you know where the diamond is now?"

"No idea," Marge lied. Convincingly, she hoped.

The woman nodded, then shrugged and plastered an unconvincing smile on her face. "Oh, well," she said. "At least it was found. That's the main thing." And she started to walk away again.

"Wait," said Marge, then realized that the question she wanted to ask the woman probably would go unanswered, but decided to ask it anyway. "Do you… the book you wrote, it's real, isn't it? It all happened the way you describe."

"No," said the woman after a moment's hesitation. "No, I just…" She seemed on the verge of saying something, but then thought better of it. "I have a very vivid imagination, and the story of the Pink Lady simply captured that imagination, that's all. It's fiction, Mrs. Poole, nothing more. You being a librarian should recognize a piece of fiction when you see it."

"Oh," said Marge, feeling slightly disappointed.

She watched as the authoress got back into her car, and quickly drove off.

12

Dinner that night was a collective affair, with the entire Poole clan gathered around the table, set up outside on the deck.

Odelia and Chase were there, of course, and Marge and Tex and Gran, but also Uncle Alec, along with his girlfriend Charlene, and even Scarlett had decided to drop by and keep us company. So it was safe to say that things proceeded in a lively way, as they usually do when the entire extended family comes together to share a nice meal.

Tex had done the honors, which was the kind of news no one likes to receive when sitting down for dinner, but the doctor had done his best, and with a little help from Chase the two men had managed to cook up a nice batch of… spaghetti bolognese, which happens to be Chase's specialty, and also just about the only dish he's mastered in the thirty-two years he's been a guest on this planet.

"I think you really should try to expand your culinary skillset, Chase," said Gran as she tried in vain to eat the spaghetti while still looking like a lady. I could have told her that spaghetti is one of those dishes it's not very pleasant to eat in the company of others, since it not only involves a lot of acrobatics of the mouth but also slithers about to such an extent you can't eat it without the use of a bib. And we all know that a bib makes any person, unless he's an infant, look like a complete fool. Lucky for us, cats don't eat spaghetti. We limit ourselves to the meatballs Chase likes to serve with his signature dish.

"What are you talking about?" said Uncle Alec, whose lips were a bright glistening red from all that bolognese sauce. "The man is a genius."

"Actually it was Dad who took care of the main food prep today," said Chase modestly. "I just stood by to lend him a helping hand."

"Nonsense," said Tex magnanimously. "You did most of the work, and I can't thank you enough… son."

"Thanks," said Chase happily as he pronged a string of spaghetti and started working it into his mouth then chewing it down with visible and audible relish.

"I mean, you don't expect your wife to eat spaghetti all her married life, do you?" Gran continued laying out her argument, undaunted by these interludes. "You should buy him a good cookbook, honey," she told her granddaughter. "Make it a birthday gift, so he can't claim he didn't get it, or miraculously 'lost' it."

"I already have all the recipes I need on the internet, thank you very much," said Chase, "and I intend to start going through them one by one. Isn't that right, babe?"

"Absolutely," said Odelia, who was clearly not yet tired of her hubby's spaghetti making skills.

"I found this YouTube channel called 'Top Chef in Thirty Days' and I'm starting with the first video tomorrow. I'll be preparing a different dish every day. I'm calling it my thirty-day challenge."

"Well, I just hope you've got an ambulance on standby," said Gran.

"Oh, but Chase is going to get a helping hand from me, isn't he?" said Tex cheerfully as he raised his glass of wine in honor of his son-in-law—the future 'Top Chef.'

"Oh, God," Gran grunted. "You mean we all have to eat—"

"Ma!" Marge interjected.

"Food! I was gonna say food!"

"I think it's great," said Scarlett. "This spaghetti is to die for, Chase. It really is."

"Stick around a couple of days," Gran muttered. "You might just get what you want."

"So what's going on with the Pink Lady?" asked Charlene, eager to change the topic of conversation. She might be a big fan of her boyfriend, but of her boyfriend's mother, not so much. But then Gran has that effect on a lot of people.

"The Pink Lady is now safely tucked away where no one will ever think to look," said Odelia.

"In our bedroom, behind the portrait of my gnome," Tex volunteered.

"Dad!" Odelia cried. "You can't tell anyone that!"

"Yeah, Tex, what's the point of all this secrecy if you're going to blab about it to anyone who will listen?" asked Uncle Alec with a frown.

"I'm sorry," said Tex, his cheeks a little flushed. "We're all friends and family here, though, right?"

"Still," said Uncle Alec. "The walls have ears, buddy. So better keep it under wraps, okay?"

"Fine," said Tex as he settled back in his chair and took another swig from his wine.

"Max, don't you think it's strange that Tex is drinking wine?" asked Dooley.

"And why is that?" I asked.

The four of us were ensconced on the porch swing, our usual spot when the family gathers together of an evening.

"Well, he's a doctor, isn't he? And shouldn't doctors set a good example by not drinking and not smoking?"

"It's just one glass of wine, Dooley," said Harriet. "There's no harm in that, is there?"

"He's already on his second glass," said Dooley, "and look, he's pouring himself a third one!"

"So? One or two glasses won't hurt anyone."

"Dooley is right, though," said Brutus as he studied the doctor closely. "This is already his third glass of wine, and yesterday he drank four during dinner, and he drank a beer while we were watching that Marvel movie together, the one about the guy who looks like a flea. He's either called Superflea or Fleaman—not sure."

"I really can't tell those Marvel movies apart anymore," said Harriet. "To me it's just one big movie, and a very boring one. I'd much rather watch something with an actual story. Something romantic."

And while Harriet and Brutus discussed the merits and demerits of Marvel movies, I watched Tex take a sip from his third glass of wine, then take another, bigger sip, and finally, while he thought no one was looking, drain the whole glass in one go!

"I think Tex is an alcoholic, Max," said Dooley now, who'd watched the same spectacle unfold. "I think he's one of those closet alcoholics, the ones nobody knows are alcoholics until it's too late."

"Do you really think so?" I asked as Tex grabbed hold of the bottle and poured himself a fourth glass!

"They call them functioning alcoholics, on account of the fact that they can keep functioning as if nothing is wrong, but meanwhile they're hiding bottles of liquor all over the house and taking sips whenever they think nobody's watching. I'll bet that Tex has a bottle of Johnny Walker tucked away in the bottom drawer of his office, and in between two patients he takes a snifter."

I laughed. "A snifter! Where did you pick up that word, Dooley?"

"General Hospital," said Dooley proudly. "Doctor Franklin was a closet alcoholic, until one day he was so drunk he accidentally took out a person's liver while he should have taken out his spleen—or was it the other way around?"

"You can't just take out a person's liver or spleen, Dooley," said Harriet. "Everybody knows that."

"Yeah, you can't take out a spleen or liver without putting another one in its place," said Brutus.

"Well, he took out something he shouldn't have taken out and the person died and that's how everyone found out he was an alcoholic. And if Tex isn't careful, the same thing is going to happen to him."

We all stared at Odelia's dad now, whose face was flushed, and even his crop of white air had a pink tinge—or maybe I was simply seeing things.

"I think we need to organize an intervention," said Brutus. "Because Dooley is right. Doctors and alcohol don't mix. What if he accentually kills a person on his operating table?"

"Tex doesn't operate," I pointed out. "He's not a surgeon." But Brutus was right. If Tex was turning into one of those closet alcoholics, an intervention probably wasn't a bad idea.

"First we need proof," Brutus continued. "We can't just go around accusing the guy of being an alcoholic. We need to dig out his bottles and show them to the others, otherwise they won't believe us."

"Huh," I said. "That's an excellent idea, Brutus."

"Why, thank you, Max," said our friend, looking inordinately pleased with this compliment.

"So what's going to happen to the Pink Lady now?" Charlene was asking. The topic seemed of particular interest to her, which wasn't that strange, since the discovery of a million-dollar diamond on her beach had stirred up quite a big ruckus in town.

"I called around," said Uncle Alec, extensively wiping his lips and leaving red smudges on the white napkin, "and discovered that the insurance company that insured the Pink Lady is still in business. They're sending a guy over first thing tomorrow to come and take a look at the stone. And then we'll know more."

"Were they happy?" asked Scarlett as she daintily lifted a single strand of spaghetti to her lips and bit off the tip, then chewed it with itty bitty movements.

"Happy? What kind of a question is that?" asked her friend. Gran had been watching the way Scarlett ate her spaghetti, and she was clearly not impressed.

"Well, I'm sure they never thought they'd recover the diamond. So the fact that the stone has been found after all those years must make them very happy."

"They did sound pretty excited," Uncle Alec admitted. "Well, as excited as those insurance folks ever get, of course. Sometimes I think they're trained not to show any emotion. Either that, or their entire workforce consists of robots."

"We'll all know more tomorrow," said Odelia. "We're meeting with the insurance people. They're bringing in an expert, isn't that right, Uncle Alec?"

"Yeah, some kind of diamond expert who'll make sure the stone is the real deal."

"I just experienced the most amazing coincidence today," said Marge as she darted a quizzical look at her husband, who was once again filling his glass—if I'd been counting right he was now on his fifth glass of wine!

"What coincidence, Mom?" asked Chase.

"Well, I was at the library, reading a book… about the Pink Lady! And not a non-fiction book either. This is a novel—a romance about a Sheikh and his wife, and how he gifted her the Pink Lady, and all the rest of the story. I'm only halfway through the book—it's called The Sheikh's Passion—but it's very gripping. And then when I locked up the library, I met the book's author! She was looking for me!"

"Oh, that's right," said Uncle Alec. "Dolores told me that some woman had called asking about the Pink Lady. So she sent her to the town librarian." He rolled his eyes. "I swear to God, that woman is getting more loopy every day."

"She's not loopy at all, Alec," said his girlfriend in a tone of censure. "Dolores did the right thing. Sending inquisitive people to the library is a fine practice, and one we can all learn from. In fact if more people would visit our library and read books instead of playing video games or being glued to their phones surfing social media all day and all night, the world would be a better place."

"Hear, hear," said Marge, and held up her hand, receiving a reciprocate high five from the Mayor.

"So what did she want, this author?" asked Scarlett, interested.

"She wanted to know if it was true that the Pink Lady had been found, and if I knew where it was being kept. Of course I didn't tell her, but…" She hesitated, which caused Odelia to look up at her mother.

"What is it, Mom?"

"I'm not sure," said Marge. "Just that… well, you know how sometimes you can get a strange feeling about a person, right?"

"Oh, sure," said Gran. "I have a very strange feeling about you right now, Scarlett."

"About me?! What are you talking about?" asked Scarlett, much surprised.

"The way you eat your spaghetti! You think you know a person, and then this happens!"

"I've always eaten my spaghetti this way. I like to taste it, not gobble it down like most people do—swallow it whole without chewing."

"Let Mom finish her story, you guys," said Odelia.

"Oh, it's not much of a story, really," said Marge with a light shrug. "Just… I asked her about her book, where she got the idea and if maybe the book was autobiographical, since she put so much detail into her story—almost as if she actually lived it, you know. But she became very evasive, and then practically ran off. So I don't know." She smiled an apologetic smile. "Just my silly imagination, I guess. That's what you get from being surrounded by all those books and all those stories—you start seeing things."

"No, but I'm sure you're onto something, Mom," said Odelia. "There is something very strange going on with that Pink Lady. I mean, I searched online, and couldn't find anything about how it disappeared. And now it suddenly turns up on a beach, thousands of miles from where it was last seen? It's a story I really want to get to the bottom of, don't you?"

Gran shrugged. "I just hope Scarlett will get to the bottom of her plate at some point. At the rate she's going that seems unlikely."

"Hasn't anyone ever told you it's rude to stare at other people's plates?" Scarlett countered.

"Hasn't anyone ever told you that you shouldn't play with your food?"

"Hasn't anyone ever told you not to comment on people's eating habits?"

"So who's going to Fido's meeting tonight?" asked Marge, wanting to nip a potential argument in the bud.

"What meeting?" asked Chase with a frown.

"Oh, he's holding a meeting at the Seabreeze Center to introduce his Flat Earth Society."

"That's right," said Charlene. "I saw something about that. What's the deal with this society?"

"The deal is that Fido has gone loco," said Gran. "And now the whole town is going to watch him self-destruct." She gave Scarlett a conspiratorial wink, which the latter reciprocated with a grin. Those two were clearly up to something again. "Here, let me help you with that," Gran now said, and grabbed Scarlett's plate and dumped half of it on her own plate and dug in.

"Thanks," said Scarlett with a happy sigh. "I hate to leave stuff on my plate, don't you?"

"Happy to help," said Gran between two mouthfuls.

"Fido believes the earth is flat?" asked Uncle Alec with a frown.

"Yeah, he does. And not only that," said Scarlett, "he wants us all to join his Flat Earth Society."

"I wouldn't miss it for the world," Tex said, and even though he was slurring his words a little, nobody seemed to notice.

Except the four of us, of course. But then we're cats—and cats are born to pick up little clues like that—clues no one else catches!

13

That evening, instead of our usual program, which includes wandering around town and joining cat choir to meet our fellow cats and hang out, we joined our humans to go to the inaugural meeting of the Long Island Flat Earth Society, which promised to be quite the show, if the number of attendants was any indication. Gran was right. It almost seemed as if the whole town had decided to come and take a look at this car crash in the making.

"They might be bailing on Fido the hairdresser," said Harriet as we settled in at the back of the theater, "but they're clearly dying to know what Fido the conspiracy theorist is up to."

"It's called disaster tourism, Harriet," I said. "Humans seem to enjoy watching one of their fellow human beings make a complete fool of themselves. It's one of the highlights of their existence."

"You mean like when a person trips over a banana skin and falls flat on his ass?" asked Brutus.

"Sure. It's the exact same principle."

Odelia and the rest of the Pooles had taken up position in

one of the back rows, so as not to be too conspicuous, and the rest of the theater was filling up nicely indeed.

The Seabreeze Music Center is one of the biggest theaters in town, and caters to a very diverse audience: one night there might be a rock band giving of its best and making the rafters quake, another night there might be a movie retrospective by some obscure Scandinavian auteur, and once upon a time even Charlie Dieber had graced this hall with his presence, much to the delight of hundreds or even thousands of screaming young fans.

Tonight the audience was a lot more sedate, and as far as I could tell there would be no screaming girls, or even teddy bears being thrown at the stage. Besides, even if Charlie were here tonight, he wouldn't stand for such nonsense. The kid had found religion, after all, and had gotten married, and was now singing songs about Jesus Christ, and no longer about his latest romantic conquest.

"Look who's here," said Dooley excitedly, his tail pointing in the direction of the door.

We all looked over, and lo and behold, two familiar figures had just graced us with their presence. They were Johnny Carew and Jerry Vale, the two career criminals who had, not unlike The Dieber himself, found religion, and had even joined the Jehovah's Witnesses for a short-lived stint.

"What do you think they're doing here?" asked Harriet as she eyed the twosome with marked interest. Johnny and Jerry were scanning the audience, and when their gazes had swept across the heads of the Poole family, returned, like the beam of a lighthouse, and a big smile slid up Jerry's face. It's hard for a man with a face like a ferret to look handsome, but when Jerry smiles, his innate ugliness is diminished by perhaps thirty to thirty-five percent, making his presence more or less palatable. Johnny, of course, is just a big brute, even though I know from experience that underneath that tough exterior there beats a gentle heart.

They now made their way over to where Odelia and her family were seated, and Jerry wasted no time taking a seat directly behind Marge, while Johnny took up position behind Scarlett Canyon, eyeing the latter with a touch of lasciviousness.

"Well, well, well," Jerry's opening statement began. "If it ain't the Pooles. Long time no see."

"Hi, Jerry," said Marge, and judging from her smile she was happy to see the twosome, which didn't surprise me, since Marge had always had a soft spot for the criminal duo. Once upon a time she'd even offered them employ at the library, cleaning up the archives in the basement. Of course they'd used this as an excuse to drill a hole through the library wall and into the bank next door, so they could abscond with the contents of a dozen or so safe deposit boxes and flee to Mexico.

But they'd been arrested and extradited and had served their time and were now upstanding and law-abiding members of the community once more. Or so they claimed.

"Hi, Scarlett," said Johnny with a silly grin on his face. The grin was not unexpected, and neither was the look of vertigo in the big guy's eyes, since he was now leaning over Scarlett, and had a bird's-eye view of the woman's décolletage. I must say the view of Scarlett's frontage has a powerful effect even from a frog's-eye view, so I could only imagine what Johnny was feeling now that he got the full experience.

"Do we know each other?" asked Scarlett, her demeanor far from frosty. Scarlett likes men, you see, almost as much as men like Scarlett, and Johnny might be rough around the edges, he's also a very large man, and presumably in Scarlett's mind that size translated in the kind of promise of virility any warm-blooded female likes to see in a member of the opposite sex.

"I've always been an admirer… from afar," Johnny confessed. "I'm a friend of Marge's," he explained.

"Well, any friend of Marge is a friend of mine," said Scarlett, and turned so she could carry on the conversation the way it should be carried on. It also caused that same vertiginous cleavage to shift and quiver like a blancmange, and I could see from the throbbing vein on Johnny's temple and the slight coloring of his cheeks that the effect was both immediate and devastating.

"Oh, look, Brutus," said Harriet with a little sigh. "It's love."

"Lust, you mean," Brutus grunted.

"What are you talking about?" asked Dooley with interest.

"Nothing, Dooley," said Harriet. "I was speaking in general."

"Oh, all right," said my friend, and the interaction drew a smile from yours truly.

"So what have you been up to?" asked Marge.

"This and that," said Jerry. "Say, is it true that a certain famous diamond was found on the beach yesterday?"

"And what's it to you?" asked Uncle Alec, his voice completely devoid of the warmth his sister had effected in hers.

"Just curious, Chief," said Jerry. "As a member of this fine community I feel it's important to stay up to date on what's going on."

"Of course you do," said the police chief, and didn't hide the skeptical note in his voice.

"So I couldn't help but notice how you dropped by Gems World this afternoon," Jerry continued, now addressing Odelia.

"You did?" said Odelia, sounding surprised. "I didn't see you."

"Well, I saw you," Jerry said with a little grin. "So did your visit have anything to do with the Pink Lady by any chance?"

"Don't answer that, babe," Chase grunted, then turned to take in the reformed crook. "What are you playing at, Vale? Why the sudden interest in the Pink Lady?"

"Cool your jets, detective," said Jerry. "Like I said, I'm just expressing a natural interest in the goings-on in my own town."

"Yeah, right," Chase said.

Jerry directed himself at Marge again. "So where is the stone now?"

"That's none of your business," said Uncle Alec.

Jerry's eyes narrowed into slits. "I sense a lot of hostility, Chief, and I can tell you right off the bat that this is both uncalled for and frankly a little disappointing." He spread his arms. "We're all friends here—and is this the way to treat a friend? Eh?"

"Friends don't break into banks and steal stuff," Uncle Alec pointed out.

"Cross my heart, those days are behind me, Chief," said Jerry, now exuding earnestness, which didn't really become him. "So where is the stone now, Marge? Safe and sound at Gems World?"

"I'm sorry, Jerry," said Marge. "But I have no idea where the Pink Lady is right now."

"And even if she knew, she wouldn't tell you," said Marge's husband. Tex's face was flushed, and Dooley's words about the man's drinking habits now returned to me.

"He's drunk, Max," Dooley whispered in my ear. "He's hiding it well, just like a true alcoholic, but he's completely wasted."

"I'm afraid you're right, Dooley," I said with a frown.

I mean, I'm not my humans' keeper, but the Pooles are all very near and dear to me, and it frankly pained me to see Tex in his current state of obvious inebriation.

"I'm telling you, he's going to take out someone's kidneys one of these days," said Brutus, "and that person won't be happy."

"If he took out a person's kidneys that person would be dead, Brutus," I said. "So they wouldn't be able to complain."

"Well, let's hope so, cause if they do complain, Tex will lose his license, and then what? He'll have to get a job selling typewriters door to door."

"Do people still use typewriters?" asked Dooley.

"I doubt it," I said.

"So let's just make sure Tex doesn't lose his license, then," said Brutus, with a sense of logic I found hard to dispute.

"Here we go," said Harriet when suddenly Fido Siniawski walked onto the stage and a hush descended upon the room.

Everyone turned to face the front. The show had begun.

14

"He looks nervous," Dooley remarked, in reference to everyone's formerly favorite hairstylist.

And indeed Fido did look nervous—in fact he looked terrified.

"Someone once said that the number one fear for humans, even more than the fear of death, is the fear of speaking in public," Harriet said.

"Is that so?" I said.

"Yeah, apparently the thought of having to talk to an audience is terrifying for most people." She shrugged. "Don't ask me why. Just another one of those human foibles, I guess."

Harriet didn't have any fear of speaking in front of an audience. In fact the opposite was true: it was impossible to drag her off a stage whenever she had the opportunity to mount it.

"So where is Buster?" asked Brutus, glancing around.

And as if summoned by the mention of his name, suddenly Buster made a beeline for us, and took up position next to Brutus. He was panting slightly. "Sorry I'm late, you guys," he said. "What did I miss?"

"Nothing," I said. "Fido hasn't started yet."

And judging from the fact that the hairdresser still stood there, looking like a deer in the headlights, and not a single word had rolled from his lips yet, I had the impression he'd never get going.

"Tell us about your flat earth!" suddenly a voice called out from the crowd.

"Yes, yes," said Fido, his voice sounding awkward and squeaky. "Thank you, Jack. As we all know, people have been told that the earth is round."

"That's because it is, you muppet!" another voice called out.

"Ha ha, thank you, Fred!" said Fido. "But now the latest scientific research has proved that this common theory is all wrong. All wrong!" he said, shifting into higher gear as he drew strength from his own convictions. "And tonight I'm going to prove this to you."

"Oh, don't bother," another heckler called out, but immediately was shushed by several of the people sitting in his vicinity.

"Let the man speak!" Charlene Butterwick said, raising her voice. "I might not agree with what he has to say," she explained in a softer tone of voice, "but that doesn't mean I don't respect his right to say it."

"Of course, sweetheart," said her boyfriend, the police chief, who was apparently still ruminating on Jerry Vale's words, judging from the annoyed glances he kept darting over his shoulder in the latter's direction. Jerry, of course, pointedly ignored the Chief's glances. If you've been operating on the wrong side of the law all your life, cops are like flies: annoying but essentially harmless.

"Look, I know what you're all thinking," Fido continued. "And I have to tell you that when I first learned of this theory, I was a little skeptical myself. But my own research on the internet has proven that we've all been lied to! The earth isn't round. The earth is in fact a flat disk, just like all the other disks that surround us. Like the sun, which is also a flat disk, and the moon, and in fact all the planets. So we need to ask ourselves: why the lies? And the simple answer is: because most people aren't ready for the truth. But the fact that you're all here tells me that you are—and that makes me very happy!"

"So what's the truth, Fido!" someone yelled.

"Well, the truth is…" Fido had walked over to a flip chart which he'd set up, and now flipped over the first page to reveal a large disk crudely drawn with a magic marker, dangling from a string. It looked like one of those UFOs from a sci-fi movie from the sixties, where the UFOs were plastic disks dangling from clearly visible iron wires. "This is the planet we're living on," Fido explained as he pointed to the disk. "And this…" He drew a square around the disk. "Is our corner of the universe." He proceeded to draw other squares next to the first one, and in each square he drew another disk. "That's right. We're not alone in the universe, folks. In fact we're all part of a gigantic network of connected disks…" He flipped over the page, and now a maze of cubicles became visible, and in each cubicle a disk was hanging, suspended from a wire. "This is the matrix," said Fido, "and we're all part of it." He flipped over another page, and the maze had grown and now looked like a beehive, with hundreds of tiny cubicles with hundreds of disks inside them. "This is the universe," he said. "This is what we are. Bees!"

Murmurs of mirth rose up from the audience.

"We're all part of a big, very big beehive, and we're the busy bees working and slaving away every day, producing…"

"Honey," a voice suggested from the crowd, to much laughter.

"Something a lot more valuable than honey. Anyone? Entertainment!" said Fido, really getting going now, as he jotted down the word entertainment on the flip chart. "The beekeepers who are masters of the universe have created this gigantic beehive for their entertainment. And they like to watch us—in fact they're watching us right now! And they're laughing, and crying, and generally looking at us the way we watch television. And that's it, folks. That's the big secret nobody's telling you. We're all actors in a big reality show— only for us it's real!"

"Oh, dear," I said quietly.

"It's worse than I thought, Max," said Dooley.

"Yeah, the guy is clearly delusional."

"Poor Fido," Buster breathed.

"Poor you," said Harriet.

"Yeah," Brutus chimed in. "Once Fido has been admitted to a mental institution, who's going to take care of you, Buster?"

"We can always ask Odelia to adopt you," Dooley suggested. "I'm sure she would do it in a heartbeat."

"Hold your horses, you guys," I said. "The patient might be sick, but there's still hope."

"And if you want to know what the beekeeper looks like —the master of our universe?" Fido was saying. "The monster that's created us and is watching us?" On the next page a crudely drawn hairy monster was featured. Oddly enough it looked a lot like… the Cookie Monster. "This is the ruler of our universe! The monster who rules us all! And his name is Roger! That's right. Roger!"

"On second thought," I said. "Maybe we should ask Odelia if she'll consider adopting you, Buster."

"That might be a good idea," Buster whispered, looking dejected as the room erupted into loud and confused chatter.

15

That night, after they'd returned from Fido's presentation, Marge had just washed her face and brushed her teeth when she came upon her husband, seated on the bed bench and staring at his favorite painting of a gnome. Gnome #16, the artist had christened it, and even though Marge wasn't exactly a big fan of the painting, she'd allowed her husband to hang it in the bedroom, but only on the condition that it be used to hide the wall safe they'd had installed. Her reasoning was that thieves would see the gnome and be so unnerved they'd immediately totter back out the window and run off screaming. Though of course she hadn't mentioned her thought process to Tex, since he'd have been devastated to know that his wife didn't share his passion for gnome art.

"Everything all right, honey?" she asked as she took a seat next to her husband and rubbed his back. She couldn't quite put her finger on it, but she had a feeling not all was well with the man she married twenty-five years ago.

"What? Oh, sure," said Tex, as if emerging from a dream. "Absolutely. Say, do you think that diamond is safe in there?"

"Nobody knows that we have it, honey," she said. "So it's absolutely safe."

"Uh-huh," he said and continued to stare at his precious gnome. It was a fat gnome, as gnomes go, and as far as Marge could tell it was also a jolly gnome, or at least his cherubic red cheeks gave the impression that he was jolly, as did the smile on his bearded little face. Still there was something sinister about him. Somehow Gnome #16 reminded her of an evil clown, only in the form of a gnome. An evil gnome, if you will. If Stephen King hadn't yet written a book about the species, she felt that he should, and would probably pack a great punch when he did.

"Let's go to bed, honey," she said as she slipped under the duvet. "I'm beat, and tomorrow is another day."

"Sure," said Tex, still continuing to not be fully present.

"So what did you think about Fido's presentation?"

"Mh?"

"Fido's presentation? If he's to be believed we're all living in the matrix, and ruled by a Cookie Monster named Roger." She laughed. "Poor guy. He's really lost it, hasn't he?"

"Yeah. Yeah, I guess you're right," said Tex, then he finally got up and joined her under the covers. "But I'll say this for him, though," he continued as he put his ice-cold feet against hers—a habit she hadn't been able to cure him from even after all those years.

"What's that?" she asked, checking if her alarm clock was set at seven.

"Well, there are things in this world that we don't know about, aren't there? I mean, the government doesn't always tell us everything, and that makes people suspicious, and wonder what else they might be keeping from us."

"Like what?"

"Like… I don't know. UFOs for instance, or aliens. Stuff like that."

She glanced over to her husband with a frown. "Aliens, Tex? Really?"

"Well, it's certainly possible that they're out there. Theoretically speaking, at least."

A tinge of worry niggled at her. "What's gotten into you all of a sudden? You never used to believe in aliens. You always said that was just a bunch of nonsense."

"I never believed in that kind of stuff before, but now I'm thinking… maybe I should." And with these words, he switched off the light on his nightstand, turned over and muttered, "Night, hon."

She blinked and her frown deepened. Usually Tex liked to cuddle before going to sleep. But then she shrugged. At least it gave her the opportunity to read some more of The Sheikh's Passion. She picked up the book, flicked off the light in the room, turned on the small reading light attached to the headboard, and was soon engrossed once again in the story of Sheikh Bab El Ehr and the love of his life: Laura.

Laura wasn't like the other women the Sheikh had met and married. For one thing, Laura wasn't a woman from his own country but hailed from the West. Her parents had moved to Khemed when she was a little girl, and had settled there, her dad an expat for a big oil company, and Laura had grown up surrounded by a culture that wasn't her own, but which she'd adopted with a passion. By the time she met the Sheikh, at a palace party her parents had been invited to, she was a beautiful young woman of nineteen, with the face of an angel and the body of a goddess, or at least that's the way the Sheikh had described her to his right-hand man Sharif the next day. Sharif had seen that the Sheikh's eyes were shining, and that the lovelight was strong in this one, and had immediately raised the alarm: the Sheikh of Khemed couldn't possibly take a western woman as his wife. That kind of break with tradition was simply out of the question.

But love listened to no reason, and the Sheikh had invited Laura to the palace under the pretext of wanting to ask her opinion about a pagoda he'd received as a present from the Chinese, and soon the two of them had been wandering around the gardens, without a chaperone, and their love had blossomed—a very unorthodox but powerful love, that had taken them both by surprise.

And by the time Marge closed the book, since the next day was a working day and she needed to get up early, she was already dreaming of a love so deep and so passionate that it consumed all.

Five minutes later she was fast asleep, spooning with her husband and dreaming of her own Sheikh, who may or may not have had a shock of white hair and the face of a certain small-town doctor with a weird penchant for garden gnomes.

So when in the middle of the night she was awakened by a strange sound, it took her a few moments to realize that the man standing in her bedroom, backlit by the full moon, wasn't the Sheikh of her dreams, but a burglar! And then she was screaming bloody murder.

16

We'd just returned from cat choir when we heard a scream so loud it cut through us like a knife.

"That's Marge!" said Harriet, alarmed. We were in the front yard when the scream rang out, which meant it must have been pretty loud, since Marge and Tex's bedroom is at the back.

So we immediately ran like the wind through the narrow patch of green that runs along the house and soon found ourselves at the back, and made our way inside through the pet flap, then up the stairs. And as we did, we came upon a fascinating scene: Tex and Marge were both sitting bolt upright in bed, and a large man was standing in front of the window, while a second, smaller man was urging him to descend a ladder which had been placed under the window. The large man was, of course, Johnny Carew, and the smaller man was his partner Jerry.

"I told you this was a bad idea, Jer," Johnny lamented.

"You idiot!" Jerry was saying. "You made way too much noise. Now look what you've done!"

"I didn't make no noise, Jer!"

"You were like an elephant in there—stomping around!"

"It's dark! I was trying to get my bearings—and then I saw that hideous monster and I got scared!"

We all glanced over to the portrait of a gnome, and I had to confess that Johnny had a point. It really was scary.

"What the hell are you doing in my bedroom?" asked Tex. A good question, I thought, and I was curious to find out the answer.

"Do you want me to scratch him, Marge?" asked Harriet obligingly. "Cause I will, you know. In fact I don't mind scratching both of them. Two for the price of one."

"No, that's fine, Harriet," said Marge. She still looked shocked but was already recovering. "Johnny and Jerry!" she said, adopting her librarian's voice—the one she uses when people return a book past its due date and have to pay a fine. "What are you doing in my bedroom?"

"That's what I just said," Tex pointed out.

"We're really sorry, Marge," said Jerry from the window. Only his head was visible, but that was bad enough. "We didn't know this was your house, did we, Johnny?"

"Jer, we can't lie to Marge. Marge is a friend, and you never lie to a friend. That's what my mama used to say," he explained to this captive audience.

Suddenly there was a loud noise on the stairs, and footsteps hurrying in our direction, and moments later Odelia and Chase came bursting into the room.

"What's going on—are you all right?" asked Odelia, panting. She was dressed in Hello Kitty PJs and looked cute as a button.

"We heard screaming," Chase explained. He was only dressed in his boxers, and looked very buff indeed.

"I'm very sorry," said Johnny, adopting a rueful tone, even wringing his big hands. He was dressed in black from head to toe, like any sensible midnight marauder would. "Better come in, Jer," he said. "We've got some 'splainin to do."

Jerry seemed reluctant to follow his friend's advice, but finally did as he was told, and I saw that he, too, was wearing fashionable black, which, as we all know, never goes out of style, and can be worn on any occasion, even when breaking and entering someone else's home in the middle of the night.

"Look, this isn't what it looks like," Jerry began.

"It looks like burglary," said Marge.

Jerry took this in, then amended his earlier statement. "Okay, so maybe it is what it looks like. But we had good reason to pay you a visit, didn't we, Johnny?"

"A very good reason," said Johnny. "You have something that belongs to us, Marge. Only it doesn't really belong to us, if you see what I mean."

"You're talking in riddles, Johnny," said Marge, still speaking in her stern librarian's voice, which was very effective, I must say.

"What's all the noise?" suddenly a voice called out from the door, and soon we were joined by a sleepy-looking Gran. When she saw the small gathering, her irritation rose. "What's up with this midnight meeting? Don't you people have jobs to go to in the morning? I know I have."

"Johnny and Jerry were just telling us why they decided to break into our house in the middle of the night," Marge said. "Go ahead, Johnny. Tell us what's going on."

"Do you wanna tell 'em or shall I?" asked Johnny.

"You better tell them," said Jerry.

"Well, it's like this…" Johnny began.

"See, that diamond you've got in that safe of yours—it's ours," said Jerry, unable to restrain himself.

"We had it and then we lost it," Johnny said, pulling a sad face.

"No, you lost it, you big dummy."

"I lost it," Johnny agreed, looking shamefaced now, as he was still twisting his hands.

"Look, I'm this close to arresting you both for breaking and entering," said Chase, "and if you don't start talking right now, and making sense, that's exactly what I'll do."

"Of course, Detective," said Jerry. "And you have every right to be upset with us—but imagine our frustration when we lost that nice Pink Lady and then suddenly it turns up in the hands of that little girl, and before we can explain to her that the rock isn't hers but ours, she hands it to her mom, and before we can talk to her, she goes and hands it to some jeweler who calls the cops!"

"The Pink Lady is yours?" asked Gran, adjusting the hairnet that keeps her nice white perm in place during the night.

"Sure, we found it fair and square, and as we all know," said Johnny, "finders keepers."

"You found that diamond? Where?" asked Marge.

"At the bank we burgled last year," Johnny said.

"You 'found' it in one of the safes you burgled?" asked Odelia.

"That's right, Miss Poole—Mrs. Poole," he quickly amended. "Congratulations on your wedding, by the way. And I'm sorry we couldn't attend. We were otherwise engaged."

"You were in prison, you mean," said Tex as he yawned then plunked his head down on his pillow again and crossed his hands in front of his chest.

"So you burgled the bank, and you found this Pink Lady inside one of the safe-deposit boxes," said Odelia, nicely reiterating the story as it had unfolded so far, "and then what?"

"Well, then we took a trip to Mexico," Jerry continued the story.

"You mean, you ran away to Mexico, cause there was an arrest warrant out on you at that point," Chase said.

"Unfortunately our trip was cut short by the very unhelpful local authorities," Jerry continued, ignoring Chase's amendment, "and so we lost the opportunity to sell the rock."

"We'd found a buyer for it—a very upstanding gentleman from Colombia," said Johnny. "But before he could hand over the cash, we were arrested and deported."

"How much?" asked Gran.

"How much what?" said Jerry.

"How much was this Columbian gentleman offering for the diamond?"

"A hundred thousand," said Jerry proudly.

There were shared looks of consternation in the room. "You do know that that stone is worth millions, right?" said Chase.

"We do now," said Jerry. "Which is why we've decided to find ourselves a new buyer."

"So in spite of the fact that you were arrested, you still managed to hang onto the stone?" asked Chase.

"Oh, sure," said Johnny. "I hid it in the sole of my shoe. Only my shoes were in my luggage, and that was confiscated when we were arrested. Lucky for us the cops didn't find the rock in my shoe."

"I hate when that happens," said Tex absentmindedly. He'd closed his eyes and looked as if he was napping. "A rock in my shoe," he explained. "Very annoying."

"So it took until last week before we got our stuff back," said Jerry, "and frankly we were surprised that the rock was still there."

"Couldn't believe our luck," Johnny said.

"So we tried to get in touch with our Columbian friend

again, only he'd recently been found hanging from a bridge in Mexico."

"Occupational hazard," Johnny explained with a shrug.

"So we needed to find a new guy. And we'd just been asking around when doofus here went and lost the precious gem, didn't you?"

"We went for a walk on the beach yesterday, and I decided to wear my lucky shoes. Only the sole must have come loose in that hot sand, and by the time I discovered I lost my sole—"

Tex laughed at this. "He lost his soul," he said. "Literally, and figuratively!"

"Okay, so a little girl found the diamond, and then what?" asked Chase.

"We've been trying to get it back ever since," said Johnny sadly.

"So how did you know it was in our safe?" asked Marge.

"Oh, Scarlett told me," said Johnny, as if it was the most natural thing in the world.

"Scarlett told you!" Gran cried.

"Sure. After the flat earth show was over—which honestly was a big disappointment, as I'd been led to believe it was a meeting of the brothers and sisters of the Jehovah's Witnesses—I asked her out for a drink, and we got to talking —she's a very nice lady, by the way, and very pretty."

"Yeah, yeah, yeah," said Gran irritably. "Get to the part where she told you about the safe."

"Well, like I said, we got to talking, and I told her how I lost that diamond, and how I didn't know how to get it back, so she said I should talk to Marge, because she had it safely locked away in her safe, hidden behind the picture of an ugly gnome." He directed a nervous look at the gnome. "I hadn't expected it to be this ugly, though."

"I'll have you know that my gnome is a work of art, mister," said Tex. "Precious art!"

"I'm going to have to have a long talk with Scarlett in the morning," said Gran. "About secrets and how we don't spill them to the first pretty face that comes along."

"Why, thank you, Mrs. Muffin," said Johnny, preening a little.

"I'd never call Johnny pretty, would you?" asked Harriet as she studied the big guy's face.

"Well, he has a certain animal magnetism, I guess," I said. "Which some women find attractive."

"I certainly don't think he's pretty," said Brutus. "But he is butch, and like Max says, a lot of ladies like butch. Isn't that so, mama bear?"

"Absolutely, papa bear," Harriet simpered.

"Oh, dear God," I said under my breath.

"So what's going to happen now?" asked Jerry, as he darted a nervous look at the cop in the room.

"By all rights I should arrest you," said Chase, but then directed a questioning glance at his wife. "What do you think?"

"I'm not sure," said Odelia, then looked to her mom for advice.

Marge, still sitting upright in bed, like a strict disciplinarian—though the impact of her iron front was slightly diminished by her unflattering flannel nightgown—seemed to waver. "Like Chase says, we probably should have you both arrested. Then again, you did try to retrieve a diamond you thought was yours."

"A diamond they stole, Marge," Gran pointed out.

"Obviously," said Marge, as she thought for a moment. "Here's what we'll do. You're not going to get the diamond, of course, because that diamond isn't yours. But I'm not going to press charges or ask Chase to arrest you, on one condition, and one condition only."

"Which is?" said Jerry, nervously licking his lips.

"The history of the Pink Lady is a little fuzzy, and for reasons that are entirely my own, it intrigues me and I want to find out more. And since you are uniquely placed with contacts in the criminal world, I want you to find out what exactly happened to the diamond between the time it went missing thirty years ago, and the moment it popped up in a safe-deposit box at the Capital First Bank in Hampton Cove of all places. Do you think you can do that for me?"

"Not just for you, Mom," said Odelia. "I'm sure that the people the diamond belongs to are dying to find out how it ended up here as well."

"You want us to play detective, is that it?" asked Jerry, rubbing his chin dubiously.

"Absolutely."

"Of course we will, Marge," said Johnny, earning himself a look of criticism from his friend.

"How much?" asked Jerry.

"What do you mean?" asked Marge with a frown.

"How much are you paying us to play detective?"

"Jerry Vale!" said Marge. "Isn't it bad enough that we caught you burgling our house?"

"All right, fair enough. So how about a finder's fee? At least we should get a finder's fee, right?"

"No finder's fee," said Chase. And when Jerry started to protest, he continued, "You're lucky Marge and Tex aren't pressing charges."

At the mention of his name, Tex opened his eyes again. "You know, Fido just may have a point. The Cookie Monster could be ruling the world."

"Go back to sleep, Tex," said Gran with a disgusted gesture of her hand. "You're drunk."

At the mention of the D-word, Marge and Odelia frowned, and directed a curious look at the good doctor. But Tex had closed his eyes again, and was now snoring like a practiced lumberjack.

"I guess we'll be going then," said Jerry, and headed to the window.

"You can take the stairs," Marge said, her expression having softened now that she knew she'd added Jerry and Johnny to the family payroll as her own private detectives.

"Gee, thanks, Marge," said Johnny.

Jerry directed a final, longing look at the portrait of the gnome, probably the only time anyone who wasn't Tex had ever looked at that ugly munchkin that way, but then his shoulders slumped and he followed his friend out of the room, and soon both crooks were stomping down the stairs.

"What a night," said Gran, voicing everyone's opinion on what had definitely been an eventful evening.

"Next time you really have to let me arrest them, Mom," said Chase, who had the air of frustration any cop would feel when he comes this close to collaring two criminals and then is told that he can't.

"I know, Chase, and I'm sorry," said Marge. "But I really want to get to the bottom of the mystery of the Pink Lady, don't you?"

She'd directed her question at her daughter and son-in-law, and they both nodded.

"I have a feeling there's probably a great story there," said Odelia.

"Absolutely," said Marge, and glanced over to the nightstand, where a very large book was lying. And when I hopped up on the bed to satisfy my own curiosity, I saw that it was titled, 'The Sheikh's Passion,' written by Loretta Gray.

Next to Marge, Tex was still snoring away. The man

might be Marge's own sheikh, but he certainly wasn't very passionate.

Which reminded me that his was another case we urgently needed to take in hand.

Humans. Even when they reach adulthood they never stop causing trouble, do they?

17

The next morning, Dooley and I decided to take a walk into town. I wanted to see how Fido's performance had affected his standing in the community, and if perhaps it had had a positive effect on his business. It wasn't entirely inconceivable, after all, that people would now flock to his hair salon, to find out all there was to know about a Cookie Monster named Roger, who seemed to hold the world's fate in his hairy paws—when he wasn't snacking on cookies, that is.

"Do you think Johnny and Jerry can be trusted, Max?" asked Dooley as we sauntered along the sidewalk, passing the paperboy who was aiming newspapers at every porch he passed with unerring accuracy. It was a skill that must have taken him years to develop. Until one of the papers sailed through an open kitchen window and must have landed in a pot of steaming soup, for mere moments later a very irate-looking lady appeared, her face splattered with tomato soup and shaking a very angry fist at the kid, who made sure he pedaled out of reach as fast as he could.

"I'm not sure, Dooley," I said. "They are two crooks, after

all, and being crooks seems to be in their blood at this point, and it must be very hard for them to reform now, after all those years of following the criminal path."

"I hope they can reform, because Scarlett really seems to like Johnny."

"What makes you think so?" I asked, surprised. I'd seen firsthand how Johnny had taken a liking to Scarlett, which wasn't so hard to imagine since most men of a certain age took a liking to her, falling frequently and fast for her allure. But it was only very rarely that Scarlett reciprocated that liking.

Dooley pointed in the direction of the corner of the street, where a cozy little patch of green had been fashioned by placing a bench underneath an old tree. On that bench Johnny and Scarlett were now sitting, and they were gazing lovingly into each other's eyes, clearly discussing something other than the interest rate policy of the Federal Reserve.

"I think it's sweet," said Dooley. "It proves that there is someone out there for everyone—even Johnny."

"Do you think there's someone out there for Jerry?" I asked. It was hard to imagine that anyone could fall for a man with the face of a rodent.

"I'm sure there is," said Dooley, that eternal optimist.

We'd reached Main Street, and as we passed by Fido's hair salon, we saw to our dismay that a sign was hanging on the door that announced that the shop was closed.

"Apparently Fido's speech didn't provide his business with a boost," I said.

"I hope Buster is all right," said Dooley.

We gazed at the storefront for a few wistful moments, mentally saying goodbye to a business that had gone bust, and then moved on.

Our next stop was the General Store, where our friend Kingman holds sway, and since so much had been happening lately, I felt it wouldn't be such a bad idea to schmooze a little with the voluminous feline who always seems to know what's going on in town, sometimes before the people involved themselves.

"Hey there, Kingman," I said by way of greeting. The large cat was taking up a large swath of public real estate by occupying a prime spot on the pavement, and didn't even lift his head in greeting when we walked up to him.

"Fellas," he said lazily. The sun was out in full force, as it often is in our corner of the world, and obviously Kingman didn't mind working on his tan a little.

"Did you hear what happened last night?" I asked, referring, of course, to the disastrous speech Fido had given to the people of his town.

"Yeah, I heard all about it," said Kingman. "Sorry I couldn't be there, guys, or cat choir. I had some important business to attend to."

"What business?" I asked. I'd wondered why Kingman would skip cat choir. Usually he's one of its fixtures, along with Shanille, the director, and all of our other friends and acquaintances.

"Oh, this and that," he said vaguely. "Looks like Fido has finally burnt his final bridge, huh? He closed his shop this morning, after having been open one hour, and then he took off for a destination or destinations unknown, I'm afraid."

"Where did he go?"

Kingman smiled. "I can't fool you, can I, Max? Okay, so Buster dropped by to say goodbye. He says they're off to California. To a place called Mount Shasta. According to Fido it's a very spiritual place, full of his kind of people, whatever that means."

"Fido moved to California? That was quick."

"What do you mean?"

"Well, after last night's disaster I suggested to Odelia she talk to Fido, and suggest a trip to Mount Shasta. It's the Flat Earth Society's headquarters."

"Now why would you go and do a thing like that, Max?"

"I didn't think he'd pick up on it so quickly. Actually Dooley gave me the idea."

"Me?" asked Dooley, much surprised.

"Yes, you. With your idea about a rich family that swaps places with a poor family. In Hampton Cove Fido is just one guy calling in the desert, making him feel special, and having the effect of strengthening his convictions. Over there he'll be one of many—just another cog in the machine." I shrugged. "I just hope it'll make him put things in perspective."

"And I hope you know what you're doing," Kingman said. "Cause after the cold reception his little speech received, Fido clearly felt that he was no longer welcome here, so I doubt whether he'll ever come back." He sighed. "And of course he took Buster with him. I'm really going to miss that fella."

We spared a moment for Buster, and I had to admit I felt a pang of regret. Buster had been a part of our lives for such a long time. I just hoped my gamble was successful.

"Look, I don't know about you guys, but I'm hungry," said Kingman, as he made a concerted effort to raise himself up from the sidewalk and move inside the store and into the cooling shade. Once there, he proceeded to gobble down a couple of nuggets from his bowl, then sat back, produced a tiny burp and said, "Dig in, fellas. I feel generous."

We could hardly believe our luck, since Kingman isn't always so forthcoming with his kibble, and so we didn't need to be told twice and dug in with relish.

"Great stuff," said Dooley. "We should tell Odelia to buy some of this for us, Max."

"It's something new. Wilbur got it in last week. Tastes great, doesn't it?"

I had my mouth full of kibble, so I couldn't immediately respond, so I simply nodded my agreement. It was, indeed, some pretty good stuff.

"Okay, you twisted my paw. I'll tell you what's going on," suddenly Kingman said. "Wilbur's found himself a girlfriend, okay? And so now I don't know what to do. I mean, on the one hand I'm happy for the guy, obviously."

"Obviously," I echoed, still savoring the taste of that fine kibble.

"But on the other hand… What if she's not a friend of cats? And what if this becomes serious and she decides to move in and kick me out?"

It was the eternal dilemma of a cat: some people like cats, such as there are the Pooles, and of course Wilbur Vickery. But others hate cats with a vengeance. And there doesn't seem to be a position in between. Either it's a full-blown love affair between man and beast, or it's an unreasonable hatred that can't be remedied.

"Who is she?" I asked, much surprised that Wilbur had found himself a girlfriend. The man is like the anti-catnip for women. He repels them, if you see what I mean.

"Oh, some writer he met," said Kingman.

"A writer?" said Dooley. "I didn't know Wilbur could read."

"He can read," said Kingman, "but he doesn't believe in books. He feels they're a waste of time."

"So how did he land himself a writer girlfriend," I asked, "if he doesn't even like reading books?"

"I'm betting he probably lied his ass off and told her he's some kind of latter-day Shakespeare."

"He lies to get dates?"

"Always. It only takes one date for them to catch on,

though. So it surprised me when he went on his second date last night." He made a face. "So you understand I wasn't in the mood to go and listen to Fido's crazy ramblings, entertaining though they must have been. I was too busy worrying about Wilbur's date trying to convince him that all cats are evil and need to be chucked out and driven back to hell whence they came. Wilbur had invited her back to our place, you see, and had actually cooked a meal, so that told me things were getting serious. And it wasn't a disaster either. The man had lit candles, and had cooked a nice lobster dinner for the lady. And I was on my best behavior, of course, hoping to make a good impression and not get kicked out when she moves in."

"Well, that's great, Kingman," I said. "Sounds like a really exciting time for your human, and for you, of course."

"And it was, until it all went south."

"Why, what happened?"

"She began by telling Wilbur that she really liked where their relationship was going, and how she thought he was just great, and yadda yadda yadda. And so then they're on the couch, after dinner, you know, and things start heating up."

"How did they heat up?" asked Dooley with interest. "Did Wilbur forget to turn down the thermostat?"

"He means they started kissing," I explained.

"Oh, kissing," said Dooley, his eyes wide with excitement. "Well, that must have been exciting for you, Kingman, to watch your human kissing!"

"Not so much," said Kingman dryly. "In fact the moment they started getting hot and heavy I left the room. I just couldn't watch. And so I decided to jump on the bed and take a nap, figuring at some point the lady would leave. Only suddenly they come barging into the room, and they're on the bed, and they're still kissing and breathing heavy and all, and so at this point I'm getting panicky, so I jump off the bed and I'm trying to figure out a spot that's safe from these crazy kids, but then she pushes Wilbur away, collects herself and says, 'I'm sorry, Wilbur, but I can't do this.'"

"Can't do this?" I asked.

"'Can't do this.' So 'Huh?' pretty much sums up Wilbur's entire reaction, and mine, too, I guess. 'No, I can't go through with this,' she says and abruptly starts buttoning up her blouse, gets up and walks out. Moments later the door slams and Wilbur turns to me and says, 'What just happened?' So I gave him a shrug and told him, 'You struck out, my man.'"

"Maybe she had second thoughts," I said. "It happens, you know. She thought she liked where things were going, until suddenly she didn't."

"Wilbur did mention that the only topic of conversation that seemed to interest her was that Pink Lady. And since he figured she was into diamonds, he'd embellished things a little and had told her during their first date the day before yesterday that he knew all about the Pink Lady. That in fact he was the godfather of the girl that had found the stone on the beach."

"And is he? Her godfather?"

"Of course not. And I think she got hip to the fact when she mentioned the girl's name and it didn't ring a bell with good old Wilbur."

"Ouch."

"Yeah."

"So how did they meet?"

"She came into the store the day before yesterday to buy shampoo, and so they got to talking, and one thing led to another…"

"So has Wilbur heard from her since last night?"

"Nope. He tried calling, he tried texting, but nada. She froze him out."

"Poor Wilbur," said Dooley with feeling.

"So look, Max," said Kingman, giving me a serious look. "I feel for the guy, you know. He's going a little nuts right now. He's sent her like a hundred texts already, and he's left about a thousand messages, and if he keeps this up she'll probably go to the cops and have him arrested for stalking or harassment or something. So maybe you could ask Vesta to sit down and talk to him?"

"I don't know about that, Kingman," I said. "Gran and Wilbur went out on a date once, too, and it didn't end well. So she's probably not the best person to give him advice about his love life."

"Yeah, I guess you're right. So maybe Odelia? Or Marge? Marge is a book person. Maybe she can give him some hot tip that will turn this thing around."

"But I thought you'd be happy to be rid of the woman?" I said. "There's a fifty-percent chance that she hates cats, and that means you're out, Kingman."

"I know, but look at the guy."

We all looked at the guy. He was sitting slumped behind his conveyor belt, listlessly scanning items, and looking like something Kingman had dragged in.

"He's lovesick," I said.

"How sweet," said Dooley with a smile.

"So talk to Odelia or Marge, will you? Tell them to give Wilbur some advice. Cause if this keeps up, life with him will be a living hell." He shook his head. "And to think it all looked so promising."

"I'll talk to Odelia," I said. "What's the girlfriend's name?"

"Um, Loretta something," he said. "Loretta... Gray?"

I frowned. Somehow the name sounded familiar.

18

*O*ur next stop was the doctor's office. But since we didn't want to announce our visit, we decided to sneak around the back, and to this end we snuck down the blind alley that leads to the houses that face the back of Tex's place of business. You see, Tex has one of those nice little city gardens, which isn't really much of a garden at all, but a couple of paving stones and grass surrounded from all sides by buildings. The only way to reach it is through the door of Tex's little kitchen, or at least that's the only way for humans to reach it. But as you may or may not know, cats are more agile than your garden-variety biped, so we jumped the dumpster that usually lines the back wall of that blind alley, then hopped up onto the wall, made our way over to the low roof of the next house, and then it was simply a matter of following along until we'd reached that small patch where Tex likes to sit with a cup of coffee and a newspaper on any given day, at least when he's run out of patients to see.

He wasn't sitting there now, though, which told us that he was probably busy inside, offering medical advice to some human in need, and as we hopped down, and then stealthily snuck up to the window, we soon found ourselves in the position that we could look into that small kitchen.

"The bottles will probably be in his office," Dooley said. "He wouldn't keep them in the kitchen where everyone can see them."

"So how do we get into his office?" I asked.

"Couldn't we ask Gran to spy on her son-in-law? She could sneak in when Tex is out and search his office."

I stared at my friend. This was an avenue of thought I hadn't pursued, and it sounded a lot easier and less stressful than what we were doing.

Then again, it was too late now. We were there, and I was adamant to find out what was going on before Tex accidentally cut out someone's spleen or liver or, God forbid, their heart or lungs.

And as we sat there, glancing into the kitchen window, and seeing no sign of liquor anywhere, suddenly a large pigeon landed in the little tree in Tex's city garden and regarded us censoriously.

"Hey, cats," the pigeon said. "Looking for food, huh?"

Why is it that the first thing anyone thinks when they see a cat is that we're looking for food?

"For your information, we're not looking for food," I told the large pigeon. "In fact I could probably tell you the same thing. Aren't pigeons always looking for something to eat?"

"I resent that, cat," said the pigeon. Then it made that cooing sound that pigeons are so famous for, flew down to the ground and pecked at a piece of bread that was lying there.

"We have a strong suspicion that one of our humans is an alcoholic," Dooley said. "So we're trying to collect evidence, so his wife and daughter can stage an intervention."

"Not Doc Poole?" said the bird, for the first time giving

the impression that he might be useful and not just a nuisance.

"Do you know Tex?" I asked.

"Oh, sure. He's the reason I'm here right now. He saved my life, you know."

"Saved your life?"

"Absolutely. I owe that man a big debt of gratitude. In fact I tell anyone who will listen that Doc Poole is by far the greatest human of his kind. A true hero to any pet facing a medical issue."

"How did he save your life, Mr. Pigeon?" asked Dooley.

"Just call me Sam," said the bird, his frosty demeanor a thing of the past now that he'd discovered we had a mutual friend in Tex. "Well, I recently hurt my left wing, see. I accidentally flew into a window and it hurt like hell. In fact it hurt so much I couldn't fly anymore, and so I just figured that was that, you know. It's hard for a pigeon to go through life without the capacity to fly. So I just sat here one day, feeling sorry for myself and generally figuring the end was near, when suddenly the Doc saw me, and picked me up and inspected me and said, 'What seems to be the trouble, little fella?' Those were his exact words," said Sam, a smile on his face at the recollection of that magical moment. "So I told him my wing was hurting and I couldn't fly, and you know what he did?"

"I have no idea," I said, not wanting to spoil Sam's story by giving away the ending, which I figured was probably a given, since he'd just proven to us that he could, indeed, fly.

"He inspected my wing, said it was probably broken, then took me inside, put me under some kind of machine, and said that my wing was broken. And so he put my wing in what he called a splint, and then kept me in that small space next to his office for the next two weeks, hand-fed me, fetched me worms and other delicious grub, and nursed me back to health, if you please! And the upshot was that when he took off that splint, I could fly again!"

"Amazing!" said Dooley, who'd been so engrossed in the story that he'd practically forgotten to breathe.

"Yeah, and so I told a couple of my friends, and then they told their friends, and now whenever one of us is in some kind of trouble, we all come here, and Doc Poole treats us and makes us well again. The man is a miracle worker, I can tell you that, and he does all this out of the goodness of his own heart, and without asking for anything in return."

"Did you hear that, Max?" said Dooley. "Tex is a miracle man."

"Yeah, I heard that, Dooley," I said. "But what I don't understand is why we're only hearing about this now."

"Well, anyway, I gotta fly," said Sam. "But if you see Doc Poole, tell him I said hi, and that I'm sending over a badger tonight who got something in his eye. Toodle-oo."

"Toodle-oo," I said as we watched Sam take flight and disappear from view with a few powerful strokes of his now fully healed wings.

"Amazing, isn't it, Max?" said Dooley. "And here we thought that Tex is a closet alcoholic, and all this time he's actually a closet Dr. Dolittle!"

"Yeah, that is pretty amazing," I agreed. Just then, the sound of a loud argument came from inside the kitchen, and when we looked through the window, we saw that its participants were none other than Tex and Gran, and from the sound of things, their discussion was more than a little heated!

19

"Tex, you have got to stop doing this to yourself!" Vesta was saying. She didn't like raising her voice, but sometimes that's what it took to get through to her stubborn son-in-law.

"I know," said Tex, looking miserable. He was leaning against the kitchen counter, a cup of hot java in his hand and taking an occasional disconsolate sip. "But how can I?"

"Look, if you don't stop, someone is bound to find out sooner or later, and then what?"

"I'll think of something," said the doctor as a pained expression crept up his face.

"Think of what? How will you ever be able to face your patients again? If you'll even have any patients left, that is. Which I'm pretty sure you won't."

"No one can know, Vesta," said Tex, a pleading note creeping into his voice. "Why can't this simply be our little secret, huh? I'm not doing anyone any harm, am I?"

"You're making promises you can't keep." Tex's mother-in-law shook her head and a sound of exasperation escaped her lips. "Why I ever agreed to keep this a secret, I don't know. I should have told Marge the day I walked in on you and caught you red-handed."

Tex looked up in alarm. "You haven't told her, have you?"

"No, I haven't, though by all rights I should. Don't you think your wife is entitled to the truth? Or your daughter?"

"I can't tell them," said Tex stubbornly. "At least not yet."

"If not now, when? You've gotta give me something, Tex. It's hard for me to sit out there in that office and keep a straight face while basically telling your patients a bunch of lies."

Tex groaned. "I know, I know. Do you think it's easy for me? I have to sit there and listen to all of their… stuff."

They were both quiet for a moment, then Tex just happened to glance out the kitchen window and suddenly cried, "Oh, no!"

Vesta looked up at this, and when she saw that two cats were seated outside on the windowsill, and had presumably heard everything with their very keen ears, she arranged her features into an expression of grim determination. "Looks like you're in for it, buddy boy. If they know, the whole town knows—or at least the cat contingent." She opened the window to let her cats in. "How long have you two been sitting there and how much have you heard?"

"We've been sitting here since you two started arguing," said Max, "and we heard every word you said." He directed a curious glance at Tex. "So what's going on?"

Both cats looked up at her, eager to find out more, but since Vesta had sworn a solemn oath not to divulge her son-in-law's secret, and she intended to keep her promise, she said, "I'm sorry, fellas. But I'm afraid my lips are sealed."

Dooley directed a keen look at her lips. "They look fine to me," he said.

"I promised Tex I wouldn't tell anyone, and I'm not going to break that promise now."

"But… you have to tell us, Gran," said Dooley, who clearly couldn't imagine a world in which Vesta didn't tell her cats all.

"I'm sorry." She glanced up at Tex, who was looking like death warmed over now.

"What do they say?" asked the doctor in a small voice.

"They've heard everything, but they have no clue what we were talking about," she said and watched as relief vied with worry on the man's face.

"Maybe we should tell them," he said finally. "After all, they're bound to find out sooner or later."

"Are you sure?"

He bit his lip for a moment, then nodded. "Maybe it's for the best. But ask them to keep it to themselves for now. I'm not ready to tell the world yet."

"All right," she said, and placed a comforting hand on the man's back. "If you say so." So she took a deep breath, and turned to her cats, who were staring at her with wild anticipation in their eyes. "You probably already know that Odelia's dad is facing a huge problem."

"We know," said Dooley, with appropriate solemnity in his voice. "He's an alcoholic."

"Wait, what?"

"Yes, we've seen how much he drinks, and we know he's in line for an intervention," Dooley continued. "Only question is, where are we going to send him?"

"Exactly," Max agreed. "The Betty Ford clinic must be very expensive, and after the whole house remodel I don't think we've got that kind of money left in the family coffers. So maybe we're going to have to settle for one of the less established but also less expensive places."

Vesta shook her head and pressed her eyes closed for a moment. "Who have you told about this… alcoholism business?"

"Well, um… everybody," said Max.

"No, we didn't tell…" Dooley thought for a moment, then smiled. "No, Max is right. We told everyone."

"In other words, the whole town now thinks that Tex has a drinking problem."

Tex looked up at these words. "What?"

She turned to her son-in-law. "The cats think you are an alcoholic, and they've told everybody."

"Oh, no!" said Tex, slapping a hand to his brow.

"It's all right, Tex," said Dooley, placing a comforting paw on the man's arm. "We're here for you. You're going to get through this, with a little help from your family."

"Yes, Tex. You just have to be strong and try to kick this awful habit," Max chimed in, also placing a helpful paw on the man's arm and starting to knead it gently.

"Why are they doing that?" asked Tex, staring down at his arm.

"They're telling you to be strong, and that they're here for you," said Vesta with an amused smile.

"I'm not an alcoholic, all right?!" Tex cried, shaking off both paws and turning on the cats.

"But… we saw how you drank no less than five glasses of wine last night during dinner," said Dooley.

"And how you behaved so strangely when your house was burgled by Johnny and Jerry," added Max.

"They saw you drink five glasses of wine last night and now they think you're an alcoholic," Vesta quickly translated the cats' words for human consumption.

"I know I drink too much!" said Tex, carefully enunciating his words, as if that would make them more understandable to Max and Dooley.

"They can hear you perfectly fine, Tex," said Vesta. "You don't have to shout."

"I'm not shouting. I just want to explain."

"Look, the thing is that Tex… is facing a midlife crisis," said Vesta.

"A midlife crisis?" asked Tex.

"What else do you want to call it?"

"Oh, all right. A midlife crisis it is. Though I'm not sure I've already reached that age."

"Tex, you're forty-eight. In fact you're probably a late bloomer as far as midlife crises go."

"What is a midlife crisis, Max?" asked Dooley.

"It's when a human reaches a certain age and starts to question if the road he or she took in life has been the right one," Max explained.

"Exactly," said Vesta. "So now Tex is wondering if he should have been a doctor after all. Cause he recently discovered that he has a different passion, and it's made him doubt his chosen profession. Isn't that right, Tex?"

"Yes, that's true," said Tex morosely as he placed his empty cup in the sink. "It all started with Sam."

"Sam?" Dooley cried. "Oh, no, he's having an affair with a woman named Sam!"

"He's not having an affair!" Vesta stressed. "Oh, for Pete's sakes. Will you listen before you jump to conclusions?"

"Sam?" said Max with a frown. "Isn't that the pigeon we just met?"

"The one who said that Tex is a miracle worker?" Dooley asked.

"Oh, so you met Sam, did you? And what did he tell you?" asked Vesta.

"Well, he said that he'd broken his wing, and how Tex fixed it up, and saved his life, and how Tex has saved plenty of other animals' lives since."

"I actually walked in on him playing the banjo to Sam, to cheer him up, and so he had to come clean. But can you see the dilemma we're facing? Our doctor here wants to transfer his medical skills from the human species to the animal kingdom, and I keep telling him that if he really wants to go through with this, he needs to think long and hard, and tell his family and his patients."

"I told you, I'm not ready to tell them yet," said Tex. "And before you two butt in, let me tell you that things aren't completely clear in my own head yet, and I think they should be, before I involve other people, all right?"

"All right, all right," said Max, holding up an appeasing paw. "Take it easy. We're not here to tell you what to do. We're only here out of concern for your wellbeing."

"We thought he was an alcoholic," Dooley repeated.

"I'm still not fully convinced that he isn't," said Max, and now took a tentative sniff from the cup of coffee Tex had placed in the sink. "Mh… " he said. "No alcohol, Dooley."

"Let me smell," said Max's friend, but soon came to the same conclusion.

"Look, Tex has been under a lot of pressure," said Vesta. "Which is why he's been drinking a little too much. But that doesn't make him a full-blown alcoholic. Far from it."

Tex dragged a weary hand through his white mane. "I've been working with patients—human patients—all of my professional life, and for some reason I just hit a point last month where I suddenly felt that enough was enough. And then Sam came along, and it felt so good to treat his broken wing and nurse him back to health. I mean, animals are so grateful for the least little thing you do for them. They don't complain that you didn't prescribe them the medication they read about on WebMD, or they don't drop by at all hours of the day or night with some imaginary disease they think they might have developed. And they certainly don't accost you at Costco when you're standing at the checkout counter, and strip down their pants to show you the suspicious mole they discovered that morning. I mean, humans can be so… exasperating, while animals are the exact opposite. So I've been giving this a lot of thought, and I'm dropping my license and becoming a vet."

Both Max and Dooley stared at the doctor, then Dooley said, "He is an alcoholic, Max. A raging one."

"No, I think he's lucid right now, Dooley," said Max. "I don't think he's under the influence."

"But… he can't give up his license. What are his patients going to do?"

"They'll find another doctor," said Vesta. "Plenty of talented physicians in the world to take Tex's place. Isn't that a fact?"

"Oh, sure," said her son-in-law. "Some young whipper-snapper will jump at the chance to take over my practice."

"But we already have a vet," said Dooley.

"And we don't need a second one," Max added.

"Yes, we hate Vena, and we like Tex," Dooley explained. "And if Tex becomes like Vena, we'll have to hate Tex, too, and we don't want to hate Tex, do we, Max?"

"No, we want to keep on liking Tex, and keep on hating Vena."

Vesta rolled her eyes. "This is all getting very, very complicated." That's what you get, of course, she thought, when you promise to keep a person's secret a secret. "Look, nothing has been decided yet. So you two don't go blabbing until Tex has decided one way or another, all right?"

"All right, Gran," said Max and Dooley in unison.

"I mean it. Not to Harriet, not to Brutus, and not to any of your other little friends."

Both cats looked pained at having to make such a promise, but finally nodded dutifully.

"Good. Though I still think you should tell your wife and your daughter, Tex."

"I will—when I'm ready," said the doctor, stubborn as ever.

Just then a loud voice called out, "Yoo-hoo! Doctor Poole? Where are you, Doctor Poole?"

Tex emitted a tired groan. "Ida," he said. "Just what I need right now." He was referring to Ida Baumgartner, one of his most loyal patients.

Vesta patted the man's back as they left the kitchen. "At moments like these I think becoming a vet is not such a bad idea after all, son."

20

I have to confess I found this all very difficult. A cat's natural instinct is to go blab about anything they pick up over the course of a day, and now we'd specifically been told to curb our inclination to spread this hot bit of gossip far and wide—tough! So I think Dooley and I could be excused for coming away from this meeting feeling more than a little dazed and confused.

"There's something I don't understand, Max," said my friend once we were back on the sidewalk and trotting along.

"There's a lot I don't understand, Dooley," I admitted.

"Okay, so Tex is a doctor of humans, right? I mean, he's a human doctor and he doctors humans?"

"I guess that's a correct assumption, yes."

"So, doesn't a doctor for humans have different qualifications than an animal doctor?"

Dooley probably meant a doctor for animals, since there are probably very few animals who get to be vets. On the other hand there are probably human doctors whose patients would argue that they're actually animals, but that's a different discussion, and one we don't need to go into at this point.

"What I'm trying to say," said Dooley, trying to make his meaning crystal clear, "don't they go to different schools and get different degrees and all that?"

"I think so—why?"

"Well, I don't think Tex can simply switch, you know. I don't think he can simply get out of bed one day and say: from now on I'm going to be curing animals, not humans. I think first he'll need to go back to school and get a degree in veterinarianism. Or is it vegetarianism?"

"I think the correct term is veterinary medicine," I said. "And you're absolutely right, Dooley. You can't just go from being a medical doctor to being a vet. Tex will have to go back to school."

"At his age that won't be easy. Studying is hard, Max—or so I've heard."

"Yeah, and I can't imagine Tex sitting amongst a bunch of teenagers while they teach him how to dissect a frog—or whatever it is they do at those dreadful institutions."

I'm being unnecessarily hard on vets, of course, and if I have caused offense, I apologize. Look, it's not that I actually hate Vena, our resident vet. It's just that I don't like it that every time we visit her she finds some excuse to prick me with a needle. It's not much fun for me, but judging from the look on her face it seems to be a lot of fun for her, which is where our notion that vets are actually closet sadists comes from. Though that look could be also a look of concentration, of course, or maybe even satisfaction that she's helped another pet—or maybe Vena's is simply one of those faces that naturally smile when in repose. At any rate, Tex was on the verge of a very big change in lifestyle: from being the town's respected doctor, he might go to being a middle-aged college student, while drawing the town's ire for leaving his patients high and dry.

"I wonder what Gran is going to do," said Dooley musingly.

"What do you mean?"

"Well, she's Tex's receptionist right now. So is she still going to be his receptionist when he becomes a vet?"

"Gran's future employment is not what worries me, Dooley," I said. "It's that Tex won't have any income for the foreseeable future, and they still have a lot of bills to pay for the work on the house."

Recently Marge and Tex's house had been inadvertently destroyed by an inadequate builder. And even though the insurance had paid out, there was still a lot of stuff they'd had to pay themselves. Like new furniture and a new kitchen and even a new bathroom. And then there was Odelia and Chase's honeymoon they had chipped in for, along with the rest of the family.

"We better hurry," I said. We had a meeting with the Pink Lady's insurance people scheduled, after all, one for which we didn't want to be late. Even though the very last thing I was interested in at that moment was to meet with an insurance person. It just goes to show how powerfully the news of Tex's midlife crisis and subsequent career change had impressed us.

We arrived at the house, where the auspicious meeting was to take place, and entered through the pet flap as usual. Harriet and Brutus were already there, and so were Odelia and Chase, seated at the dining room table, patiently awaiting the arrival of the insurance folks. In the middle of the table stood the small jewel box, and in it, I presumed, was the Pink Lady, awaiting further developments and possible inspection.

"What took you so long?" asked Harriet with a touch of irritation.

"Oh, we had some business to attend to in town," I said.

"What business?" asked Brutus with a frown.

"Oh, this and that," I said vaguely, since I couldn't think of an excuse right then.

"We discovered a secret," Dooley announced with a proud smile.

"Dooley!" I said.

"Don't worry, I won't tell them. That's because it's a secret," he explained to Harriet and Brutus, who were staring at my friend with open-mouthed anticipation.

"A secret?" said Harriet. "Well, what is it?"

"I can't tell you," said Dooley happily, "but it's a big secret. A very big secret. And once you hear what it is, you're going to be so surprised. So, so surprised."

"Dooley…" I groaned.

"But I can't tell you what it is right now," he continued, "because we made a promise to a certain person that we wouldn't tell anyone, so we're not telling anyone."

"Oh, don't give us that crap," said Brutus. "Tell!"

"I'm sorry but I really can't," said Dooley, and closed his lips ostentatiously, then mimicked locking them and throwing away the key.

"Don't be like that, Dooley," said Harriet, moving closer to my friend and giving him a gentle nudge with her shoulder. "I'm your oldest and dearest friend. You can tell me anything. You know that, right?"

But Dooley shook his head.

I didn't feel like coming to his aid, for he'd maneuvered himself into this untenable position all by himself.

"Oh, Dooley," Harriet said with a little sigh. "Sweet, sweet Dooley…" She gave him a nudge with her head. "Do you know I've always thought you're the sweetest , nicest cat I know?"

At this point Dooley looked as if the top of his head was just about to come off, but he was still staying strong.

"Oh, but Dooley, you're hurt!" suddenly Harriet cried out, and pointed to a speck of dust on my friend's shoulder.

"That's just a speck of…" I began, but Harriet was already planting a delicate kiss on the spot.

"There, that should make it all better," she purred.

Brutus was eyeing this spectacle with unreserved astonishment. It's probably not a nice experience to have to watch the love of your life pant little kisses on other cats, but then Harriet would argue that this all served the greater good.

"Oh, but Dooley, you have a cut!" she said, this time pointing to the cat's neck. And once more she planted a little kiss just so.

Dooley, who was sitting on a crate of dynamite, ready to explode, suddenly burst out, "Tex is tired of being a doctor and he wants to become a vet! There, I said it." He turned to me. "Does that make me a bad person, Max?"

"No, it doesn't, Dooley," I said with a little eyeroll. Harriet had put him on the spot, and I imagined if she'd handled me the same way she'd just handled Dooley, I might have spilled the beans, too. She has her ways, Harriet does.

Harriet was glowing with pride, but Brutus said, "Tex wants to be a vet? Are you sure?"

"Oh, absolutely," said Dooley. "He and Gran told us the whole story. How he's fed up with his patients showing him weird-looking moles at Costco, and how pets are a much more grateful clientele, and how he dreams of becoming a vet, and never having to see another human patient in his life. Oh, and the reason he drinks so much is because he can't decide whether to go through with his midwife crisis or not."

"Midwife crisis?" asked Brutus. "What are you talking about?"

"He means a midlife crisis," I said. "Tex hasn't been feeling well lately. And so he's been drinking more, even though he says he's not an alcoholic, and he's been thinking about making a big and sweeping life change, only he's afraid that if he does, the consequences will be devastating. So he hasn't told anyone, except Gran, and now he's trying to decide what to do."

"Tex a vet," said Harriet.

"I hate vets," Brutus grunted. "Sadists, every last one of them. Always with their needles and their poking and their prodding."

"Not Tex," said Dooley. "Tex will be a very nice vet, the kind of vet who doesn't poke you or prod you or stick you with a needle."

"Oh, he'll stab you with needles and all the rest of it," said Brutus. "Just you wait and see. Now he's acting all nice and friendly, to put you off guard, but once he's got you strapped to his table, he'll go to town on you. You don't have to teach me vets. I've seen them all and they're all the same."

"Not Tex," Dooley insisted. "Right, Max?"

"I don't know, Dooley," I said. "I haven't seen him in action yet, so it's too soon to tell."

"He would never hurt anyone," Dooley insisted stubbornly. "Sam said he saved his life, and he's saved the lives of plenty of Sam's friends, and Sam says Tex is a miracle worker. He's like Dr. Dolittle, and Dr. Dolittle would never hurt an animal."

"What are you babbling about?" asked Harriet, her sultry demeanor now fully a thing of the past. "Who is Sam?"

"Sam is a pigeon we met in Tex's city garden," I explained. "He suffered a broken wing and Tex nursed him back to health, so now he's extremely grateful and told all his friends, and they've all dropped by at various intervals to be treated by Tex."

"So who's paying for all of these treatments?" asked Harriet, that mercantile streak that runs through her veins once again manifesting itself.

"No one, I guess."

"He's doing all of that stuff for free," said Dooley.

"Well, he shouldn't," said Harriet. "If he's going to be a vet, he needs to learn how to ask for money."

"I'm sure that if he becomes a vet—which is still a big if," I said, "he'll ask for money just fine. And if he doesn't, Gran will. Look," I continued, "you can't tell anyone about this, you hear?"

"Of course not, Max," said Harriet sweetly. "We won't tell a living soul, isn't that so, smoochie poo?"

"Sure," said Brutus with a grin. "Not a living soul."

Oh, dear. I had a feeling Dooley had just let the cat out of the bag.

Just then, the doorbell rang, and Odelia went to answer it, after darting a quick glance at her husband. Chase sat up a little straighter, and when a tall man walked in, holding a brown leather briefcase in his hand and eagerly glancing around, presumably looking for the Pink Lady, we all jumped up on the couch, to have a first-row seat to the show.

The Pink Lady was finally going to be handed over to its rightful owner.

21

"Is this it—she—her?" asked the tall man. He wore spectacles and had a russet little beard going, and possessed a sort of bouncy, peppy energy, like a puppy. A gangling human puppy. Behind him, a second man had entered at a slower pace. He was short and stocky and had a more meditative air about him, his dark eyes flitting about the room, taking everything in. He had a thick mustache and a weathered sort of face, as if the elements had had their way with it from an early age, and he looked exactly how I imagined a Pinkerton detective would have looked traversing the wild West and collaring the scum of the earth.

"Yes, that's the Pink Lady," said Chase as he handed the little box over to the tall guy.

The insurance man opened the box and regarded the diamond in silent admiration. Sunlight hit the stone just so, and splashed a burst of iridescent sparkles on his face, and his mouth actually opened to release a small 'Oh!'

Turns out even tough and hardened insurance people aren't immune to the allure of an exceptionally pretty pink diamond.

The second man now spoke up for the first time. "A good afternoon, one and all," he grunted as he went to stand next to the tall man and checked the stone. No little 'Oh' sound of admiration escaped this man's lips, and in fact his hardened features didn't even change expression at the sight of the Pink Lady. He clearly wasn't impressed.

"So you're the expert?" asked Chase, who'd gotten up and walked around the table to greet the men.

"I'm the expert," said the tall man, who'd taken out a small loupe, and was studying the stone from up close and personal.

"I'm Oscar Godish," said the Pinkerton detective. "I work for Milestone Partners. And this is Dwayne Late, the world's foremost diamond expert." He'd hooked his thumbs into the waistband of his pants, and I found myself wondering where he kept his revolver and his Pinkerton badge.

"So what's the verdict, Mr. Late?" asked Odelia as the tall man shook his head.

"It's an exquisite specimen," he murmured reverently. "Flawless in spite of the unfortunate conditions to which she was subjected. Carried to Mexico and back in the sole of a shoe. Callous, Mrs. Poole. Extremely callous."

"Yes, it's a small miracle the stone survived."

"Found in a pile of sand on the beach, mh? It doesn't bear thinking what would have happened if that little girl hadn't found her when she did."

"Probably washed away into the deep and never seen again," said Mr. Godish.

"So who is the rightful owner?" asked Chase.

"Well, Sheikh Bab El Ehr, ruler of Khemed, was the original owner," said the insurance man as he placed the stone back in the box, "but he died in 2015. His eldest son Bab El Ghat became the new ruler upon the death of his father, and so he's the rightful owner of the Pink Lady."

"What about the Sheikh's wife Laura Burns?" asked Odelia. "The stone was set in the engagement ring her husband the Sheikh gave her, so isn't she the rightful owner?"

"According to Khemed law upon marrying the Sheikh his wives lose all claims to any personal possessions they may have accumulated up to that point, so even though Sheikh Bab El Ehr gave her that ring, it remained his private property when the marriage was officiated. So this little beauty," he said, tapping the jewel box affectionately, "will finally go home to Khemed."

"You know, Mayor Butterwick called me this morning," said Odelia, "and she suggested that we turn the handing over of the Pink Lady into an official event at Town Hall. That way you'd be able to meet the girl who found the diamond, and perhaps give her some kind of token of the Sheikh's appreciation—her parents would also be there, and the media would of course be represented."

"Oh, absolutely," said Mr. Late. "You mean like a photo op with Mr. Godish and myself?"

"It would give you an opportunity to officially thank the Wynns," said Chase.

"I think that's a great idea. Don't you, Oscar?"

"Sounds swell," said Mr. Godish without much enthusiasm. Then again, your Pinkerton detective just likes to get the job done without too much fuss—or some Town Hall shenanigans.

"Isn't that nice, Max?" said Dooley. "There's going to be a big going-away party for the Pink Lady and we'll all get to say goodbye."

"Maybe they can thank Johnny and Jerry while they're at it," Brutus grunted.

"Oh, of course," said Dooley. "Johnny did keep the stone nice and safe in his shoe, after all."

"Oh, Dooley," Harriet sighed.

"The full story is still not completely clear to me," said Odelia, the reporter in her stirring itself. "The stone disappeared, when exactly?"

"I'm afraid that part of the history of the Pink Lady is a little opaque, even to me," said the world's foremost diamond expert. "Either the diamond was lost or stolen, nobody seems to know for sure. But at any rate, it was thought lost forever, until it resurfaced in Hampton Cove—one of those mysteries of history, I guess. And perhaps we'll never really know what happened."

"Any idea how it ended up in a safe deposit box at Capital First Bank?" asked Chase.

"You looked into that side of the story, didn't you, Oscar?"

Oscar Godish nodded. "I talked to the bank manager. A Mr. Brady Dexter. And he told me the safe it was stolen from belonged to a man named Craig Bantam. Unfortunately Mr. Bantam died a couple of years ago, and so far I haven't been able to contact his relatives." He shrugged. "Look, the most important thing for Sheikh Bab El Ghat is the safe return of the Pink Lady. He's not looking to launch a full-blown investigation into the circumstances of the diamond's disappearance or reappearance. So as far as we're concerned, Mr. Kingsley—our work is done."

Odelia looked a little disappointed by this. She, of course, had every reason to get to the bottom of the mystery surrounding the precious rock. She had an article to write, after all.

"But if you do manage to find out what happened, perhaps you'll give the Gazette the scoop?" she asked now.

The little man's eyes narrowed. "I don't do scoops, Mrs. Poole," he said in a measured tone that left no room for doubt as to how he felt about journalists. "No scoops, no snoops."

After the duo had left with the Pink Lady, Odelia turned

to Chase. "No scoops, no snoops—that was a dig, wasn't it? A dig at me, because he thinks I'm some kind of snoop?"

"Or maybe he simply meant it in general," said Chase. "At any rate, the diamond is finally gone, and now we can rest easy again."

"Maybe you can rest easy, but I want to find out what happened, and if I understood that insurance guy correctly, I won't have to expect any help from him."

"Isn't your uncle still involved? He said he was going to try to get to the bottom of this business, wasn't he?"

Odelia gave her hubby a grateful smile. "Thanks, babe. Looks like I know who to call first."

"Odelia, before you do that," I said. "Can you talk to Wilbur Vickery? He went on two dates with this woman Loretta Gray, and since she walked out of their last date she hasn't been answering his calls or messages and he's feeling really down in the dumps."

"Loretta Gray?" said Odelia. "Why does that name sound familiar?"

"The book your mom is reading," said Chase.

"What book?"

"The book about the Pink Lady. The writer is also named Loretta Gray."

"Do you think they're the same person?"

"Probably. She's definitely in town, since your mom met her yesterday, so maybe she's dating Wilbur now?"

"Dating Wilbur," said Odelia, then shivered slightly. "Imagine that."

"Oh, and we just found out a big secret about Tex," Dooley piped up, "but since it's a secret we're not supposed to tell anyone. Just thought you'd want to know."

Odelia slowly turned to Dooley, then said, "Dooley, is this a joke?"

"No joke," said Dooley with a smile. "A secret."

Odelia now took a seat on the sofa right next to my friend, looked him straight in the eye and said, "Tell me everything. Right now."

22

"You know, Max," said Dooley, "instead of becoming a vet, maybe Tex should become a hairdresser. Now that Fido is gone he could take over the salon."

"I think that's a great idea, Dooley."

We were traveling in Odelia's car in the direction of the police station, and we were just passing by Fido's salon. A For Sale sign had been placed in the window, a sad testament to the notion that Buster might never return, and would spend the rest of his life with the flat earthlings of Mount Shasta, California. Okay, so maybe that hadn't been my best idea ever. You can't hit them all out of the park!

"I still can't believe Dad would want to stop being a doctor and become a vet," Odelia said. She hadn't responded well to Dooley's news.

"But he seems to be very good at it," I said. "Sam the pigeon was very satisfied with the services Tex offered him. If it hadn't been for your dad, in fact, Sam might be dead right now, so that's at least one pigeon's life saved."

"No offense, Max, and I know this Sam is probably a good friend of yours—"

"More of an acquaintance than a friend, but go on."

"—but I care more about the health and safety of the people of Hampton Cove than that of a single pigeon."

"Oh, but Tex saved a lot more lives than just Sam's," said Dooley. "In fact if Sam is to be believed, he's like Hampton Cove's very own Dr. Dolittle." He turned to me. "I just thought of a joke, Max. Should I say it?"

"Go ahead," I said.

"Tex could call himself Dr. Poolittle. From Poole and Dolittle—get it? Poo-little."

"Oh, I get it, Dooley," I said with a small smile.

"Dr. Poolittle indeed," Odelia grumbled, gripping the steering wheel a little tighter. Judging from the whiteness of her knuckles Dr. Poolittle would find no support from his daughter in his new endeavors, even though I had no doubt she would watch his future career with interest.

"So when are you going to talk to Wilbur?" asked Dooley. "And offer him some relationship advice?"

"Frankly I don't give a hoot about Wilbur or his relationship," Odelia muttered as she resolutely steered the car right past the General Store, where presumably Wilbur was still bombarding his latest conquest with hundreds of messages, and set a course for the police station instead.

Life is about priorities, after all. When you have a story to write about a precious diamond, and your dear old dad has decided to burn his career to the ground, the love life of Wilbur Vickery has to take a backseat. Collateral damage, I think some people would call it.

We'd arrived at the police station, and Odelia parked her car, then got out, allowing us to hop down to the ground to follow her inside.

We passed Dolores, the precinct's crusty dispatcher, who

waved to us in greeting while barking into her phone, "No, ma'am, this is the police, NOT the DMV!"

And then we found ourselves in Uncle Alec's office. The big man was behind his desk, looking a little frazzled. His hair was standing in all directions—or at least what little hair he had left on his wide cranium, and when we entered he was on the phone, gesturing for his niece to take a seat. "No, Charlene, I don't know when the Sheikh will arrive. Oh, he's already here? Well, he sure as heck didn't tell me. An official reception at Town Hall? Do you really think that's necessary? Keys to the city? Are you sure... Yes, Charlene. If you think it's a good idea." And after adding, "Yeah, love you, too," he hung up. Somehow that last sentence hadn't sounded as loving as it could have.

"Did I hear you correctly?" asked Odelia. "Is Sheikh Bab El Ghat in town?"

The Chief nodded, then dragged ten weary digits through the devastated area that was his scalp. "The town council wants to organize a reception for the Sheikh, the whole nine yards—champagne, canapés, invite the whole town, the works. As if I don't have enough on my plate already."

Odelia gave her uncle a strange look. "I just had the Sheikh's insurance guy at the house and his expert, and they didn't mention anything about the Sheikh being in Hampton Cove."

"Maybe they didn't know. Guys like that don't exactly like to make their travel plans known to the whole world. No, yeah, the guy arrived late last night. Wants to meet the Wynns and thank them personally for finding the stone. He's staying at the Star—apparently renting a suite on the top floor for him and however many of his wives he decided to bring along on this trip." He tugged at his nose. "I just hope no nutters get it into their nut to camp out in front of the hotel hoping to catch a glimpse of the Sheikh or, worse, decide to try and shoot the guy."

"Shoot the guy? Why would anyone want to shoot the guy?"

"Because that's what people do!" said the Chief, throwing up his hands. "They like to shoot at stuff, just because they can. Now why are you here? Did we have a meeting? I can't remember."

"I'm here to talk about the investigation into the disappearance and recovery of the Pink Lady. I want to find out how that diamond got into that safe deposit box at the Capital First Bank."

"Uh-huh. Okay. So I talked to the bank—"

"And they told you that that safe belonged to Craig Bantam."

The Chief stared at his niece. "How…"

She smiled. "Oscar Godish told me."

"Who's…"

"The Sheikh's insurance guy. Works for a company called Milestone Partners."

"Okay. So your Mr. Godish is correct. The safe deposit box was registered to a Craig Bantam. Now, Mr. Bantam died a couple of years ago, but he had a daughter, and that daughter has kept on paying for that safe, which is why your best bet would be to talk to the daughter. I'd do it myself, but nobody has asked me to investigate, and frankly I don't have the time or the manpower to launch a full-scale investigation into that darned rock. Honestly I'll be glad to be rid of the thing."

"No worries, Uncle. I've got plenty of time, and the best thing is that nobody has to tell me to investigate this strange business. I *want* to investigate it—in fact I can't think of anything else!"

"Good for you," grumbled her uncle. "And if this Bantam

woman gives you any grief, just flash them this badge." And he pushed a small badge across his desk in Odelia's direction.

Odelia stared at it for a moment. "What's this?"

"I just thought I'd make it official that you're a police consultant—not a cop, mind you, but still working for me."

"Why, thanks," she said, and looked extremely touched by this sign of trust.

"Oh, and also there's this," said Uncle Alec, and slipped an envelope across the stable, following the same trajectory as the badge.

Odelia frowned as she checked the contents of the envelope. "What…"

"If you're going to be an official police consultant, you're going on the payroll. On a freelance basis."

"But… this is too much," said Odelia, probably the first time in the history of the world anyone had said that after receiving remuneration for services rendered.

"It's fine. I discussed it with Charlene, and considering all that you've done for this town, we think it's only fair. And now you better scram, honey. I've got a ton of work, a Sheikh to protect from the crazies, and I don't even know where to start!"

"Uncle Alec?" said Dooley. "When do we get our badges as official consultant's consultants?"

"And our paycheck?" I added. "You can pay in kibble—we don't mind."

Odelia smiled, but decided not to translate our words this time. Her uncle had enough on his plate already. And besides, have you ever seen a cat wear a badge? Where would they even pin it!

23

"Don't you think you should have told Uncle Alec about what happened with Johnny and Jerry last night?" I asked once we were back in the car.

"No, I don't," said Odelia. "We gave our word we wouldn't tell my uncle, and I intend to keep it."

"Do you really believe they'll go out of their way to investigate what happened to that diamond?"

"You never know, Max. Something I learned from my mom: she always sees the good in people. Maybe Johnny and Jerry will surprise us."

"They definitely surprised your parents when they broke into their bedroom last night."

We were on the road to Craig Bantam's daughter, Craig being the man who rented that safe deposit box, and I wondered what we'd discover. This diamond business was easily as baffling as any mystery I'd ever encountered, and so far I couldn't see where it would lead.

"We saw Johnny and Scarlett kissing on a bench," Dooley announced. "Do you think that's part of his investigation, Odelia?"

Odelia looked thoroughly surprised by this development. "Johnny and Scarlett? No way."

"Oh, yes," I said with grim satisfaction. "So it looks like our boys aren't exactly taking their investigation seriously."

"He could be investigating Scarlett," Dooley said. "And hoping she will give up a few clues."

"Scarlett will give up something, all right," said Odelia, "but it won't be clues."

"It might be a clue how to get into her—"

"Max!" said Odelia.

"—confidence!" I finished. "She is, after all, Gran's best friend, so maybe this is all part of a scheme to get their hands on that stone somehow."

"If it is, they're barking up the wrong tree, since by now that stone is safe and sound in the hands of the Sheikh."

Just then, Odelia's phone chimed, and she placed an earbud into her ear, then pressed a little button. "Odelia Poole."

Unfortunately we couldn't hear what was being said, but we could of course follow the conversation by listening to Odelia's side of it, which spoke volumes. "Yes, I personally delivered the Pink Lady into the hands of Oscar Godish and Dwayne Late," she said, then listened for a moment, before saying, "They were at the house maybe an hour ago—two hours, tops." More talk was going on at the other end of the conversation, then Odelia cried, "Are you serious?!" and turned to face me in the rearview mirror.

"Looks like something's wrong," I told Dooley.

"Probably Johnny and Jerry. Have you noticed, Max, that often when something goes wrong, those two are involved?"

"I'm not so sure it's them this time."

"Of course," said Odelia. "No, I understand, Mr. Maroun. Absolutely." When she finally disconnected, she just stared before her for a few moments, then said, "The Pink Lady's gone missing again."

"What do you mean? Did those two guys lose it?"

"No, looks like they're the ones that took it. That was Sharif Maroun on the phone, the Sheikh's right-hand man. Late and Godish were supposed to deliver the diamond to the hotel half an hour ago but they never showed up. They've tried calling but they've gone off the grid. So they called Milestone Partners and turns out Godish sent in his resignation this morning. He no longer works for them. And as far as Dwayne Late is concerned, far from being the world's foremost diamond expert, he's one of Godish's contacts—an ordinary jeweler from Queens." She sighed. "Looks like we've been had, boys. Played for suckers."

"But why? Why would they take a million-dollar diamond?" asked Dooley. Odelia actually turned her head to give him a look, and so did I. After a few moments, the penny dropped. "Oh."

"So what's going to happen now?" I asked.

She shrugged. "They're not blaming me. I did the right thing. They should have been more careful—or Milestone Partners. Anyway, they've called my uncle, and the police are looking into it."

"No scoops, no snoops," I said, reiterating the words of the insurance guy. "Looks like he really played us."

Odelia looked distinctly unhappy, but since there wasn't anything she could do right now, she pressed on in the direction of the house where Craig Bantam's daughter lived, and five minutes later was ringing that lady's bell, Dooley and I at her feet as usual, willing to lend any assistance we could. We were, after all, unbadged consultant's consultants and we took our jobs seriously.

"Mrs. Bantam?" asked Odelia the moment the door swung open.

"Bantam is my maiden name," said the woman. "These days I go by my married name—Fossard."

"My name is Odelia Poole, and I'm a civilian consultant with the local police department. We're investigating the Pink Lady diamond. I don't know if you've heard of it?"

The woman who stood before us was of the slightly rumpled kind, with a thick crop of dark hair, a round face, and dressed in a sweater and jogging pants. She looked as if we had caught her engaged in some sort of strenuous activity, since her cheeks were flushed, and a sheen of sweat covered her brow.

"Of course I've heard of it," she said cheerfully. "It's all people are talking about. Come in." And as she led us inside, she continued, "I was just doing my workout routine, so you came at the right time." She grinned. "Any excuse to take a break from that torture machine is fine with me."

We found ourselves in a cozy living room, with plenty of throw pillows covering several couches placed strategically in front of a large-screen television. Posters of ABBA bedecked the walls, and framed pictures of the four members of the group covered every available surface, from the display cabinet to the sideboard.

"I'm a big ABBA fan," she explained when she followed Odelia's look. "I think they're just great. I keep hoping they'll get back together and play a concert." She gestured to the white leather couch. "Take a seat. Can I offer you anything? I have ABBA tea, ABBA coffee, ABBA lemonade, ABBA cookies…"

"ABBA coffee will be fine," said Odelia, who's a big coffee drinker. "And maybe water for my cats. It doesn't have to be ABBA water," she quipped.

"Oh, but I have ABBA water," said Mrs. Fossard. "It's more bubbly than regular water and tastes sweeter."

"Thanks," I said gratefully when moments later a dish of

water was placed on the floor for my and Dooley's enjoyment. She was right, by the way. It was sweeter.

"So what's this all about?" she asked as she sank into an armchair with visible relish. The music blasting from the speakers was of course ABBA, and she now turned down the volume.

"So you know all about the Pink Lady turning up on the beach the day before yesterday, right?" asked Odelia, scooting forward on the couch and causing it to make squeaky noises.

"Absolutely. Imagine looking for seashells and finding a precious diamond instead. Oh, the joy that little girl must have felt!"

"So I take it you don't know about the safe?"

"Safe?" asked the woman. She took a nibble from one of her ABBA cookies, then seemed to think better of it and ate it whole. In other words a lady after my own heart.

"I like a woman with an appetite, Max," said Dooley, who'd noticed the same thing.

"Me, too," I said. I'd taken a great liking to Caroline Fossard, though the fact that she'd placed a small dish with liver pâté next to the water might have had something to do with that.

"Well, the Pink Lady was stolen from the Capital First Bank last year, and according to the information from the bank manager it was actually stolen from your safe."

The woman gawked at Odelia. "My safe? What do you mean?"

"I mean the safe the Pink Lady was stolen from is registered in your name, Mrs. Fossard."

"Oh, dear. You mean there was something of actual value in that safe? I thought it was just a pile of old junk!"

"I'm sorry—I don't understand."

"I'll tell you what happened. My dad took that safe, but he

put it in my name for some reason. But so eighteen years ago he died, and as far as he'd told Mom the only thing he kept in that safe were some old work documents and unimportant stuff. She still wanted to take a look, of course, after he died, but discovered that Dad hadn't left her the key to the safe—he'd died unexpectedly, you see—or the combination. So she went to the bank to ask them to open it and they said that since it was in my name she had to have the key. Otherwise they'd have to drill out the lock and replace it, and that would set her back three hundred bucks. So she never bothered, and then more or less forgot all about it."

"But you kept on paying for that safe. That must have cost you a lot of money over the years."

"Oh, no. You see, it was all paid in advance. Dad had arranged all that, and so Mom figured that when the money ran out, the bank would open the safe and that would be that."

"So the years passed and…"

"And some idiots burgled the bank, and stole everything they could lay their grubby little hands on. So I thought, tough luck, but I wasn't going to weep over a bunch of old documents."

"Only it wasn't some old documents. It was a precious diamond that's been missing for years," said Odelia.

"But… how in the world did my dad get a hold of a diamond?"

"What line of work was he in?"

"He was an engineer. He worked for Spark, a company that designs and builds hydroelectric power plants."

"Hydroelectric power plants," said Odelia, musing on this for a moment.

"Yeah, he traveled all over the world to build those plants. He built them on every continent, and was very proud of what he did. When I was little me and my mom would travel with him to the most exotic places. But then when I got older they decided it was best for me to stay put and go to school. So Dad just came and went, sometimes staying away for weeks at a time. Though he tried to make sure to be home for all the important stuff."

"How did he die?"

"Trouble with his ticker. He'd had a cardiac arrest on one of his trips, and hadn't been the same since. Doctors told us that if it happened again, it might be fatal, and so he decided to take early retirement, and spend whatever time he had left with his family. And he did. He lived another ten years. But then he had another episode. It all went really quickly so he didn't suffer."

"Did he ever spend time in Khemed?" I asked.

Caroline Fossard smiled down at me. "Oh, how cute is that? It's almost as if he's trying to tell us something."

"Yeah, cats are amazing creatures," Odelia agreed. "So what I wanted to ask you: did your father ever spend time in Khemed?"

Caroline drew her brows up into a frown, and thought for a moment. "I'm not sure…" She swiftly got up and disappeared into the next room. We heard a drawer open and close, and moments later she returned with what looked like a large ledger and sat down next to Odelia, placing the book on the coffee table, which also held an ABBA coffee-table book. "Mom kept this," she explained. "She wrote down the dates and destinations of every place Dad ever visited, and when he came home, he pasted pictures in here for me. It was like our family album, so we always knew where dad was when he wasn't here." She popped a pair of reading glasses on her nose and opened the book in the middle. "When did you say the Pink Lady disappeared?"

"Well, nobody seems to know for sure, but Laura Burns,

the woman whom it was given to died in 1986, and as far as I can tell the diamond hasn't surfaced since."

"1986…" said Caroline, leafing through thick pages, festooned with pictures and airplane tickets and other memories of her dad's travels. "Here we are," she said. "In 1986 my dad was in Sweden to oversee work on a new power plant, and then later in the year he was sent to…" Her jaw dropped as she turned the page and stared at the inscription. "Khemed," she said. "September to October 1986. He even took pictures." Odelia scooted over to take a look. "See? He kept his hotel bill. The International Royal in Wadesdah, which is the capital of Khemed."

Odelia held up her phone. "Can I…"

"Sure, go ahead," said Caroline, who'd put a hand to her face and was shaking her head.

Odelia took a couple of pictures of the pages where Caroline's father had documented his stay.

"I don't get this. So my dad took a diamond that didn't belong to him, and then kept it in a safe at the bank all these years and never told us? But why? Why would he do a thing like that?"

"Maybe he needed money?"

"So why didn't he sell it? Why steal it and then keep it?"

"Maybe because he discovered he couldn't sell it? It is a pretty famous diamond. Stones like that are very hard to sell. Nobody wants to touch them."

But Caroline shook her head decidedly. "My dad wasn't a thief. He just wasn't. If he took that stone, there must have been a good reason, cause he sure as heck wouldn't have stolen it."

"Who's that?" asked Odelia, as she pointed to a particular picture in the album.

"Oh, that's Ken. Kenneth Cesseki. He was my dad's go-to guy—an assistant of sorts. Real jack-of-all-trades. Ken always traveled with my dad. He was a company man. Not an engineer like my dad, but more like a fixer. He arranged the visas, and made sure the paperwork was in order and liaised with local authorities, that kind of thing."

"Is he still…"

"Alive? Oh, yes. Though I'm not sure where he hangs out these days. Back when Dad was still with us, they used to meet up all the time, to talk about the good old days. I think Dad once told us he lived in Boston." She tapped her lower lip. "I could always call Spark's HR department. He might even still be on the payroll. Guys like Ken never retire. They just keep on going, like the Energizer Bunny."

"Oh, please do," said Odelia. "I just discovered that the diamond was stolen a second time—and I really need to find out what's going on, and the best way is to dig into its past."

"I'll call them right away," said Caroline, and got up to retrieve her phone. She disappeared into the kitchen for a moment, and we heard her talking to someone.

"Maybe her dad was a crook?" Dooley suggested. "And he simply never told his family. Just like Tex never told his family that he doesn't want to be a doctor anymore."

Odelia winced. "Wait till Mom hears about this."

"Oh, but it's a secret, Odelia," said Dooley. "So you can't tell your mom."

"I'll tell her to keep it a secret," she said.

"Well, then I guess it's all right," said my friend after giving this some thought. "As long as it's a secret, it's fine."

Caroline had returned and handed a piece of paper which held the pictures of the four members of ABBA to Odelia. "This is his number. As it turns out he retired last year, though he still does odd jobs for the company from time to time as a freelancer." She smiled. "Like I said, guys like Ken never retire."

Odelia thanked Caroline profusely, and the latter made

her promise to let her know if she found out what had happened to that diamond.

"Even if it means that my dad committed a crime," she said as we were standing in the door. "I mean, I like to think he was an honest man, and I really hope that he was, but how well do you really know a person, right? And this is too much of a coincidence to be ignored."

"As soon as I find out what happened, I'll come and tell you personally," said Odelia, pressing the woman's hand warmly.

Caroline looked a little discombobulated, which wasn't surprising. She'd just discovered that her dad, whom she obviously had loved and admired, might have been involved in the theft and smuggle of an extremely precious stone. You'd be discombobulated for less!

24

"I don't understand what she sees in that guy," said Harriet as she directed a look of annoyance in the direction of the canoodling couple.

"Like you said, he's butch and built like a bull," said Brutus.

They'd been taking a stroll around the neighborhood, wondering where Max and Dooley had gone off to this time, and had ended up taking a breather in a small patch of greenery the town had provided for the weary wanderer on the corner of a nearby street. Only they hadn't had the piece of downtown greenery to themselves, but rather had discovered they were sharing it with none other than Scarlett Canyon and... Johnny.

The couple—for that was what they apparently had become in the short space of time since their first meeting—were kissing up a storm, and it seemed obvious that they really liked each other. No, make that really, *really* liked each other.

"He's big and strong but he's also a crook, Brutus," Harriet reminded her mate. "And as far as I know Scarlett is no gangster's moll."

"But he's not a gangster anymore, is he? He's reformed now."

"Yeah, that's why he broke into our house last night, because he's reformed. No, Brutus, the man is a crook, and all I can think is that this is a way for him to get his hands on that stone."

"The diamond? But Scarlett doesn't have it, does she?"

"No, she doesn't, but she might possess information about how he can get it."

"Oh, Johnny," said Scarlett in a soft purr. "You're such a great kisser."

"No, you're the good kisser, Scarlett," said Johnny.

"So maybe we can take this inside?"

"I wish I could, but me and Jer are staying in a real dump. Not the kind of place I could take a lady like yourself."

"So maybe we can go to my place?"

"Do you really think we should?" asked Johnny, suddenly reluctant.

"Why, don't you want to see where I live?"

"Oh, absolutely," said the former crook. He gazed at her reverently. "This is like a dream come true, Scarlett. It's just that…"

"Just what, Johnny?" said Scarlett, that purr in her voice having much the same effect on Johnny as Harriet's purr had had on Dooley. The prissy Persian recognized the technique, and for some reason resented Scarlett for employing it to such great effect.

"I promised Jerry I'd help him find this rock, see, and he's probably waiting for me."

"You mean the Pink Lady?"

"Yeah. Marge wants us to find out how it ended up in that safe we burgled a couple of months ago."

"Oh, Johnny, you lead such a fascinating life," Scarlett cooed.

"I can promise you right here and right now, Scarlett, that this is all behind me now. I'm done with the life of crime. It's the straight and narrow for me, I swear."

"I think it's kinda sexy to date a gangster," said Scarlett, eyeing her new conquest from beneath lowered lashes.

"Date?" said Johnny huskily. "Did you say date?" He seemed to have grown a few inches, which made him even bigger than the man mountain he already was.

"Well, do you want to date me, Johnny? Cause you just have to say the word and this girl is yours for the keeping."

"Oh, Scarlett," Johnny rasped. "Oh, Scarlett, Scarlett," he added, in case she hadn't heard him the first time. "Oh, Scarlett, Scarlett, Scarlett," he croaked, this time clasping her hands in his. And then he was wrapping her into his arms and more kissing ensued.

"Yuck," said Harriet. "I think it's time we left these two lovebirds to themselves, don't you?"

"Yeah, let's go."

Moving on, they happened to pass by the park, and decided to take a breather there. Harriet hoped they wouldn't bump into more loved-up couples. She might be a true romantic at heart, but the last thing she needed right now were kissing couples. After the spectacle they'd just witnessed, the thought of humans kissing made her sick.

"I really don't understand what the big deal is with kissing," she said. "Personally I think it's gross. Putting your tongue against the tongue of another person. Yuck."

"Yeah, it's pretty disgusting," said Brutus, making a face.

"And besides, it's very unhygienic. All that saliva that's involved, and those bacteria. There should probably be a law against kissing. It's a public health risk. I think it would be in the benefit of all of mankind if—say, what are those two doing there?"

She was referring to Dwayne Late and Oscar Godish, seated on a nearby park bench and talking animatedly with a third person, some blonde who looked familiar somehow. And then she had it. "Isn't that the writer whose book Marge is reading?" She'd seen it lying on Marge's nightstand.

"Yeah, I think so," said Brutus.

"So what is she doing with those two guys?"

And then, before their very eyes, suddenly the shortest guy, the insurance man, took out a small box from his pocket, and handed it to the writer, who gratefully tucked it away into her purse!

"Hey, they're handing the Pink Lady to that author woman!" said Harriet.

"Maybe she's the Sheikh?"

"Don't be stupid, Brutus. There are no women sheikhs. Besides, why would a sheikh meet in a public park to exchange diamonds? No, there's something fishy going on."

"So what do we do?"

"We don't do anything. We just make sure they don't see us, and we follow that diamond."

"Good idea," said Brutus approvingly.

Harriet smiled in spite of the shocking scene. "You know what this means, don't you?"

"No, what?"

"That we might be able to best Max at his own game for once."

Brutus's face lit up with a smile of such wattage it probably could be seen from outer space. "Oh, my," he said softly.

It had been far too long since they'd cracked a case, Max usually being the one who found the killer or solved the mystery, in spite of Harriet and Brutus's best efforts. But not this time!

And so when finally the trio split up, with the insurance guy and the diamond expert going one way and the author lady going another, Harriet and Brutus decided to follow the money—or at least the diamond—and were soon tailing the author through the park, tails high, and making sure they stayed out of sight, just like real detectives would.

Their mission was suddenly complicated—or simplified —by the fact that they spotted another familiar figure reposing on a bench: Marge Poole!

25

Marge, who'd been relaxing with her new favorite book, suddenly started when a loud "Pshhhht!" sounded in her ear, immediately followed by, "Don't turn around!"

"It's us," a second voice chimed in. "Harriet and Brutus!"

"Oh, hey, you guys," she said as she placed down the book. "What's with all the cloak and dagger stuff?"

"Don't look now, Marge, but to your immediate right there's that woman—the writer of that book you're reading."

So she glanced over ever so discreetly, and saw that Harriet was right: there was Loretta Gray, walking past with a certain briskness in her step, not looking left or right.

"Don't scream, Marge, but she just took possession of the Pink Lady!" Harriet loud-whispered.

Marge had no intention of screaming—in fact it would have taken a lot more than this message for her to start hollering her head off, but still she couldn't suppress a quick intake of breath. "The Pink Lady? But I thought Odelia and Chase were supposed to give it to the insurance people?"

"They did, and the insurance people just gave it to this lady."

"So now we're following her and trying to find out what's going on," Brutus added.

This time Marge did glance back, and saw that both cats were hiding in the bushes behind the bench. "I don't get it. Why would the insurance people hand the diamond to Loretta Gray?"

"I have absolutely no idea," said Harriet, "but my spider sense is tingling, which tells me that something is off."

She smiled. "You have a spider sense?"

"Not really," said Harriet with a shrug. "But I have feline intuition, which is probably even better."

"Yeah, I have feline intuition, too," said Brutus, "and plenty of alarm bells are going off in my head right now."

"Okay, so maybe I'll follow along with you guys. Cause I have to tell you that I don't trust this woman either. When I talked to her yesterday she was acting very strange, and I've been reading her book, and she knows a lot of stuff that she couldn't possibly know."

"Like what?" asked Harriet as she and Brutus emerged from the bushes and the trio got going, following Loretta from a safe distance.

"Like the fact that Laura Burns, the Sheikh's ninety-ninth wife, wasn't well-liked by the Sheikh's courtiers or by his ninety-eight other wives."

"But why?" asked Harriet.

"Because she was deemed too western. Also, according to the book Laura was the only one of the Sheikh's wives he actually was in love with."

"He wasn't in love with his other wives?" asked Brutus.

"No, he wasn't. In Khemed the tradition is that families offer up one of their daughters to the Sheikh, and when he accepts, it brings great honor to the family."

"So he collected wives like other people collect stamps?"

"More or less. Love doesn't feature into the thing. It's purely a business transaction."

"Odd practice."

"Odd?" said Harriet, peeved. "Medieval, you mean. In some countries people offer their best sheep or cow to the ruler, and in Khemed they offer women. It's barbaric, that's what it is."

"Well, apparently this is all part of the tradition," Marge continued. "At least it was until the Sheikh met Laura. According to the book he fell in love at first sight, and the feeling was mutual."

"So a wedding out of love, huh? That's better already," said Harriet. "Though I don't understand why she would marry a guy who already has ninety-eight other wives."

"So what happened then?" asked Brutus.

"Well, the wedding was an amazing affair, it lasted ten days, and people came from all over the world to celebrate with the Sheikh and his wife."

"Wives, plural," said Harriet.

"And then things turned sour, right?" said Brutus. "The Sheikh locked her up and started treating her bad?"

"No, on the contrary. As the days passed, they grew ever closer together, and there was even talk that the Sheikh would send all of his other wives away, out of respect for Laura, which would have been revolutionary. She became pregnant very quickly, and gave birth to a lovely baby girl with curly golden hair, and it completed the happiness of the newlywed couple."

"And then what happened?" asked Harriet eagerly.

"Then you came sneaking up on me from behind and told me to spy on the writer of the book," said Marge with a smile.

"But you have to tell us how it ends!" said Harriet.

"Why don't you ask that lady we're following?" Brutus suggested. "I'm sure she'll be able to tell you all about it—including why she took that diamond and what she's planning to do with it."

Loretta Gray had left the park, and was now walking along the sidewalk, Marge and her two cats still in tow, and gave no indication of being aware that she was being followed, which was just as well, as Marge was no professional detective, and she had the feeling that if Loretta just turned around, she would spot her immediately.

But lucky for her, the authoress just kept on walking, and soon was crossing the street. Marge decided to stay on her side of the street, and suddenly said, "I think I know where she's going."

"Where?" asked Harriet.

"The Star hotel."

And lo and behold: the Star came into view, and as Marge had expected, Loretta entered the hotel.

"Do you think we should follow her in?" asked Brutus.

"If you want to, we can take it from here," Harriet suggested.

"No, two cats will stand out like sore thumbs, no offense."

"None taken," said Harriet, though her expression told a different story. No one calls a Persian a sore thumb.

"What I mean is, everybody who sees you walk in can't help but notice you, Harriet."

"Oh, of course," said Harriet, her tail, which had gone half-mast, now rising swiftly again.

"Maybe I better call my brother and tell him what we discovered." But as Marge reached for her phone, suddenly she had a better idea.

26

*K*enneth Cesseki may have lived in Boston once upon a time, but these days he had opted to move a little farther afield and now resided in lovely Thailand.

Odelia probably wouldn't have minded going all the way to Thailand—she had, after all, fond memories of the time she'd participated as an undercover candidate on Passion Island, the well-known reality show—but thankfully modern technology made that unnecessary, and so we all sat in front of Odelia's screen in her new home office, and found ourselves looking at Mr. Cesseki in person, dressed in a colorful T-shirt and ball cap, seated outside on what looked like a nice beach. There were even palm fronds waving at us from time to time, as if extending a formal invitation to visit soon.

Mr. Cesseki was a man of indefinite age. He could have been fifty, but he could also have been in his early seventies. He had one of those ruddy faces you get from spending half your life in hot climes with not a lot more in the form of protection against the sun's rays than a hat and sunglasses.

His skin had that leathery look that some crocodiles like to show off with.

"Hi there," he said good-naturedly. "So you're Odelia Poole? I've read your articles, Miss Poole."

"Mrs. Poole," Odelia corrected him with a smile. "I wasn't aware I was famous all the way down to Thailand, Mr. Cesseki."

"Just call me Ken. Well, Craig lived in Hampton Cove all his life, and he was a big Gazette reader, and I guess it rubbed off on me. It's nice to keep up with the home front. When you're living as far away from home as I am these days you tend to get homesick, and reading about daily life in such a nice and cozy place like Hampton Cove makes up for it to some extent. Almost like you're there!"

"Thanks, Ken. That's probably one of the nicest compliments anyone has ever paid me."

"Well, it's true, and I'm sure I'm not the only one who feels that way."

"So the reason I'm calling you—I talked to Craig's daughter Caroline, and she told me to get in touch with you."

"Sweet Caroline. Did you know I used to dandle that little tyke on my knee once upon a time? I guess she's all grown up now."

"She certainly is."

"So what did you wanna know?"

"I don't know if you've followed the news, but a famous pink diamond turned up on our beach the other day. The Pink Lady." She waited to see if the name rang a bell, and wasn't disappointed. The man's eyebrows shot up into his cap and practically knocked it off his head.

"The Pink Lady, huh? Well, I'll be damned."

"So you have heard about that particular diamond?"

"I'll say that I have, Mrs. Poole."

"Odelia, please. So Caroline told me that you and her dad

used to work several projects around the world, and one particular project was in Khemed."

"Oh, I remember it well. Fall of 1986 and Craig and I had been summoned by the Sheikh of Khemed. He wanted to build a dam on the Nabataean River to provide electricity to the countryside. So we landed there and we're set up at one of those fancy hotels, the name of which escapes me right now, and set to work. Only we soon discovered there was a fly in the ointment in the form of the Sheikh's right-hand guy, who had a little side project he wanted to interest us in."

"A side project?" asked Odelia.

"This guy sure likes to talk, doesn't he, Max?" Dooley commented.

"And a good thing, too," I said. "Imagine if he didn't want to talk. It would make our job a lot harder."

"So what did he want?" asked Odelia.

"Well, so the guy comes to our hotel room one night, okay? And so we figured he wants to talk numbers. You know, look at the project and maybe get the ball rolling a little faster by cutting through some of that bureaucracy and red tape. But no, he had something completely different in mind. Turns out the Sheikh had recently gotten married to his hundredth or two-hundredth wife or something, and this guy clearly wasn't happy with his boss's choice of life partner. So he pretty much asked us to talk to the lady, and maybe try to convince her to come back with us."

"Come back with you? I don't understand."

"Yeah, that makes two of us. Or three. We didn't get what the guy was driving at either. But then it all became clear. Crystal clear, in fact. He wanted me and Craig to meet the lady, and have a chat with her at the hotel, ostensibly about the dam, but also about her home country. Turns out that even though she'd grown up in Khemed, her folks were actually American, and she'd gone to college in New York. And so the Sheikh's man said the lady would love the pleasure of our company for some innocent reminiscing. You know, shoot the breeze a little, and talk about the good old days when she was a student in the West. So we said sure, send her along, and he did. The whole thing felt a little off, though, if you know what I mean, but then when you're doing business in a country like that everything feels off, so it's very hard to know if things are really off, or if that's just the way they do things down there."

"So you met Laura Burns?" asked Odelia, her attention riveted, as was ours, I have to say. The guy was a very good raconteur.

He now took a sip from an umbrella cocktail and continued. "So about an hour or so later the lady drives up—yeah, Laura Burns her name was—only the receptionist called up to our room—we were sharing a suite at this point, Craig and me—and said there was someone in the lobby who wanted to see us. So we said send her on up, figuring this was probably the Sheikh's wife. And it sure was, and she was even more beautiful in person than in the pictures I'd seen."

"And so what happened then?"

"Well, nothing happened, really. We talked about the States, and she asked us what was going on with this and that, and a good time was had by all. We talked about an hour or two, and then she left, very graciously thanking us for our time, and so we figured that was that. Another notch on our belts for the mutual benefit of the project. Cause there wasn't a hair on our heads that thought anything untoward had happened."

"Just a friendly conversation between two foreign contractors and the wife of the Sheikh."

"Exactly! So we went to bed feeling pretty good about ourselves, only to be woken in the middle of the night by a persistent banging on the door of the suite. And even before

PURRFECT SPARKLE

we managed to open the door, it was busted open and an entire contingent of cops or soldiers or security people or whatever they call it down there came bursting into our room, and before we could ask what the hell was going on, they're wrestled us to the floor, handcuffed us, put bags over our heads and were carting us off!"

"You were arrested?"

"Arrested, tried and kicked out of the country, all in the space of an hour, and in the middle of the night, no less."

"But why?"

"We were hauled in front of some kind of judge, and as far as we understood from the court-appointed lawyer we were being charged with insulting the Sheikh. Turns out that it's illegal for a so-called commoner to talk to any of the Sheikh's wives. And not only had we talked to Laura, we'd been alone in a room with her, with not a single other person present, which was considered a crime. For a moment it looked as if we might be hung, drawn and quartered, but in the end the fact that the Sheikh really wanted that dam built saved our hides, and so we were exiled instead. Exiled never to set foot in Khemed ever again."

"My God, that must have been terrible."

"We used slightly stronger language to describe the experience, I can tell you."

"But didn't Laura know that it was illegal for her to associate with you?"

"She must have known, but either she threw caution to the wind, because she was so eager to talk to a couple of Americans, or she was misinformed. But that's where our Khemed adventure ended, and not a high note either."

"So what happened to Laura?"

"Well, it wasn't long after that she died."

"Jeez."

"Yeah. So I have no idea if she was sick, but I can tell you that when we met her she was in great shape."

"What was the official cause of death, do you know?"

"Nothing was communicated as such, but we heard through the grapevine that she'd suddenly gotten very ill, was taken to the hospital and died within a couple of hours."

"Died from what?"

"No idea. You have to understand that Khemed is one of those countries where everything is hush-hush. So whatever really happened to her, we'll probably never know."

Odelia chewed on this for a moment while Ken took another sip from his umbrella drink. "So the thing is, Ken, that I'm investigating the Pink Lady, specifically how it ended up in Hampton Cove."

"Oh, that's right. You wanted to ask me about that diamond, didn't you?"

"Yes, turns out that Craig kept it in a safe at the bank all these years, until the bank was burgled and the diamond was stolen, then lost again, only to be found by a little girl playing on the beach. Now I talked to Caroline, and she was as surprised as anyone that the Pink Lady would have been in her dad's safe. He'd told them the safe only contained some old documents and work stuff."

"Uh-huh."

"So do you have any idea how a diamond that used to belong to the wife of the Sheikh ended up in your colleague's safe?"

Ken took off his ball cap and scratched his scalp at this point. "Well, now, that is a darn peculiar story, Odelia. And for the life of me I can't tell you how Craig got his hands on that diamond."

"Laura didn't give it to you by any chance?"

"No, I can't say that she did."

"Was she wearing her engagement ring when she came to see you that day?"

"Honestly I wouldn't know. I'm not the kind of guy who notices that kind of thing." He pulled a funny face. "Ask me half an hour after this conversation what you were wearing and I'm sure I'll draw a complete blank. She could have been wearing her ring, and it could have been that famous Pink Lady, but I didn't pay attention and I'm pretty sure neither did Craig."

"But somehow Craig must have come into possession of that diamond."

"It sure looks that way. But I gotta tell you, Odelia, this comes as much as a surprise to me as it does to you and Caroline. How *did* Craig get a hold of that rock? It's a real head-scratcher."

"He never told you about it?"

"Nope. And to be honest, when we were arrested we were also searched, the both of us, and our luggage was confiscated, so we left that country with only the clothes on our backs and nothing more. Though later on our replacements did manage to get some of our stuff back, and also the plans we'd been working on."

"But no diamond."

"No diamond."

Odelia thought for a moment. "This is such a baffling mystery, and I really want to get to the bottom of it."

"Yeah, and I sincerely hope you do, and that you can tell me all about it when you manage to crack the code, so to speak."

Odelia was clearly disappointed, but she hid it well. "Well, thank you for your time, Ken."

"No sweat. There's nothing much for me to do here, except to drink, party and be merry, and even though that sounds like something a lot of people would dream of, even paradise gets old after a while, Odelia, trust me."

After the man had rung off, Odelia turned to us. "This is so odd, but did you also get the impression that he wasn't telling us everything?"

"He definitely gave me the impression he was holding something back," I agreed. "You, Dooley?"

"I think he was secretly in love with Laura and they were having an affair and that's why he was kicked out of the country," said Dooley. "Or maybe Laura had an affair with Ken and Craig both, and she didn't know who to choose, and then her husband found out and had her killed and her body fed to the crocodiles."

"I think your imagination is running away with you again, Dooley," I said. "But that there's something going on here that Ken didn't want us to know, that's obvious. I mean, how did Craig get his hands on that diamond without Ken knowing about it? That seems very unlikely."

"Unlikely, but not impossible," said Odelia. "Maybe Craig was up to something and didn't want to tell his colleague about it."

"Colleague and friend," I pointed out. "They kept meeting up long after Craig had retired. That sounds like a firm friendship to me."

Just then, Odelia's phone rang, and she picked up with a cheery, "Hey, Mom what's up?" She listened for a moment, then glanced down at us. "We'll be there in five minutes." The moment she'd disconnected, she said, "Mom says Loretta Gray has the Pink Lady, and she just walked into the Star hotel."

"Let's go," I said.

"The plot thickens, doesn't it, Max?" said Dooley

"It sure does, Dooley."

27

We all met in front of the Star, and I have to admit that Marge had come up with a great plan of campaign.

"So we'll go in and pretend to be Loretta's biggest fans," said Odelia, reiterating the plan.

"I don't even have to pretend to be one of her biggest fans," said Marge. "I actually am one of her biggest fans. Except for the part where she took that diamond, of course."

"And while you get her autograph and keep her talking, I'll snoop around. I like it, Mom. Simple and effective."

"I didn't know Marge had detective ambitions," I told Harriet.

"Why, you'd be surprised by the talent we've got in-house," our Persian friend said haughtily as she tilted her chin. "In fact it was our idea, wasn't it, Brutus, to follow this diamond thief, and it was also us that recognized the insurance people in the first place, and saw them hand the diamond to this author-slash-thief."

"Yeah, so if you want to give credit, it's ours," said Brutus. "Mine and Harriet's."

"Yes, Max, did you get that? This time all the credit for solving the mystery goes to me and Brutus and me and Brutus alone."

"Oh, no, absolutely," I said. "You did a great job, you guys."

"We discovered something, too," said Dooley.

"Whatever you discovered can't be as big and enormous as what we discovered," said Brutus.

"So what was it?" asked Harriet, carefully studying her nails.

"We talked to Ken Cesseki, who was Craig Bantam's colleague in 1986, and he told us that he and Craig were arrested for talking to the Sheikh's wife and kicked out of the country," I said, summing up the conversation in as few words as possible, since both Marge and Odelia were raring to go in and do their thing.

Harriet frowned. "So how did his colleague get his hands on that diamond?"

I shrugged. "Ken claims he has no idea."

"A likely story," Harriet scoffed. "Let me tell you something, Max. If you're going to interrogate a person, you need to use the proper technique, otherwise they'll just lie to you and think they're getting away with it—and it looks to me," she added as she gave me a supercilious look, "that he actually did get away with it."

"You should have waited for me and Harriet to be there," said Brutus. "We would have seen right through the guy!"

"It's very hard to put pressure on a person when you're a cat," I reminded my friends.

"And the conversation was all done through Skype," said Dooley.

"Yeah, it's even harder to put pressure on a person through Skype."

"Ken lives in Thailand," Dooley explained, "and likes to drink umbrella cocktails under a palm tree on the beach. But he says he's bored of paradise and he wants to come home and spend time in Hampton Cove, which he called a cozy little town."

"He didn't actually say he wants to come home," I said.

"No, but I'm sure that's what he meant."

"Oh, so now you're putting words in other people's mouths, are you?" said Harriet. "Way to go, Dooley."

Dooley smiled widely. "Gee, thanks, Harriet. Coming from you that's a big compliment."

"I was being sarcastic," said Harriet with a touch of acerbity.

"I don't think Dooley gets sarcasm, do you, Dooley?" asked Brutus.

Dooley gave him a look of uncertainty. "What's sarcasm, Brutus?"

But then it was time to get the show on the road, and so we followed Marge and Odelia into the hotel.

Once inside, Marge walked up to the front desk—she was in the lead now—and asked what room Loretta Gray was staying in. The pimply receptionist told her no Loretta Gray was staying at the hotel, so then it was Odelia's turn. She joined her mom at the front desk, and whipped out her snazzy new police badge and immediately the kid's eyes went wide, blushing a pretty crimson under his pimples, then hastened to say, "Oh, you mean Loretta *Gray*! She's in room two-fourteen, detective… officer… sergeant?"

"Police consultant," said Odelia in that officious voice your true cop likes to assume. It takes years of training at the police academy to master that particular tone of authority, but Odelia, even though she hadn't spent a day at police academy, had the tone down pat, which just goes to show she's an absolute natural at this cop thing.

And so moments later we were riding the elevator up to the second floor, and then were dawdling in front of room

214, Marge looking decidedly nervous now, even though it had been her plan in the first place.

"You do it," she suddenly said, taking a step back from the brink. "I'm too nervous."

"No, Mom, you're the big fan—you have to do it."

"You can be the fan, and I'll be the one rifling through her things."

"But I haven't even read the book!"

"Oh, dear," said Marge, chewing her bottom lip for a moment. Then she seemed to gather her courage, and raised her hand to knock, only to lower it again. "I'm going to screw this up. I just know it!"

"You'll be fine. Forget that we're here to get that diamond and just think of yourself as the fan that you are, meeting her big hero in the flesh for the first time."

"But it's not the first time. We met yesterday on the street in front of the library."

"Even better. That means that first awkward moment is over with, and you can pick up where you left off."

"We left off with her racing away in her car after I asked her some questions she didn't like."

"Oh, Mom," Odelia groaned, and decided to take matters into her own hands and did the knocking for her mom.

"What did you do?!"

"I knocked on the door!"

"I'm out of here," said Marge, and made to leave.

But then the door suddenly swung open and Loretta Gray appeared. "Marge?"

Marge quickly covered her nervousness with an engaging smile and said, "Loretta! Fancy meeting you here!"

"Oh, boy," Brutus muttered next to me.

Dooley, who'd been studying a spot on the carpet, asked me if I thought it was Nutella or jam or blood.

"What are you doing here?" asked Loretta, as her eyes

flitted from Marge to Odelia down to the four cats staring up at her—well, three cats, since Dooley was still studying that spot and now gave it a tentative lick.

"I think it's jam," he said.

"Don't lick weird stuff on the carpet, Dooley," I told him.

"It's not weird, it's jam."

"So I forgot to ask you for your autograph yesterday," said Marge, finally rallying round. She held up the voluminous tome called The Sheikh's Passion and practically thrusted it at the writer.

"I'm Marge's daughter," said Odelia, smiling in her most disarming way possible. "Mom told me all about your wonderful book, so I started to read it last night and it's just fantastic. I don't think I've ever read a story that has gripped me so much as The Sheikh's Passion."

"I think she's overdoing it," said Harriet. "First rule for a good detective: always play it cool."

"Yeah, she better tone it down," said Brutus. "Nobody likes to be buttered up to such an extent."

But the authoress's frosty demeanor thawed under this onslaught of praise, and she was even affecting a smile when she said, "Why, thank you. Do you want to come in for a moment?"

"We'd love to," said Marge, and stepped in, followed by Odelia and the cat contingent, with yours truly bringing up the rear.

"I'm sorry," said Odelia the moment the door was closed, "but could I perhaps use your bathroom?"

"It's through there," said the writer, and gestured to a door near the window.

"So I was hoping to find out what inspired you to write such an amazing story," said Marge, continuing in her gushing tones, which seemed to have such a positive effect on the writer.

"Well, like I told you yesterday, I'm blessed with a lot of imagination."

"But it's so true to life."

"It's all fiction, Marge," said Loretta, taking the book from her big fan's hands. "Sheer fiction, I assure you."

"But the Pink Lady is real."

"Well, yes, certain aspects of the book are loosely based in reality. Like the Pink Lady. But the rest is fiction." She'd dug out a pen and was now writing a dedication on the first page.

And as Marge talked to the author, and got her to open up about the book's inspiration, Odelia was still in that bathroom, presumably searching it from top to bottom for a certain pink diamond.

"She won't have hidden it in the bathroom," said Harriet decidedly. "She only got back twenty minutes ago, so she wouldn't have had time to look for a proper hiding place."

"It's probably in her luggage," said Brutus, indicating the suitcase that had been shoved underneath the bed.

"Or maybe in her clothes?" Dooley suggested, pointing to the closet where several dresses hung suspended from clothes hangers.

"Or maybe she has a jewel case and it's in there," suggested Harriet.

"This is hopeless," was my opinion. "This room really needs to be gone over with a fine-tooth comb, and we neither have the time or the opportunity to do that."

"Yeah, I think Marge should call the cops and get this over with," said Brutus.

"Chase would have found that diamond by now," Dooley opined. "Because he is a very good cop, and when he wants to find something he always finds it. That's the kind of cop he is."

And while my friends were arguing amongst themselves as to what the best course of action would be, my attention was drawn to the nightstand, where Loretta had put her phone, and right next to her phone lay… an envelope. I frowned as I took it in. There was a bulge in that envelope, a bulge that matched the size of a diamond. So while Marge was entertaining Loretta, and Harriet, Dooley and Brutus were talking strategy, and Odelia was presumably lifting the toilet seat to look underneath, I tripped over to the nightstand in as auspicious a way as I knew how, and with a single nail lifted the flap of that envelope. And lo and behold: a pink shimmer greeted me the moment the flap was lifted. I swallowed away a lump of excitement. So now what?

I darted a quick look over to Loretta, still talking about her vivid imagination and how it had sustained her through all of the months she'd spent writing her precious tome, and then gave the envelope a casual flick. It dropped to the floor, and since I didn't know what else to do, I took the stone that had rolled from its recess into my mouth, then quickly walked back to my friends.

"I wave wit," I said.

They all stared at me. "What's wrong with you, Max?" said Harriet. "You sound funny."

"I wave we phtone!" I said, trying to talk around the object I now held in my mouth.

"I think he's running a fever," said Brutus.

"Let me feel your brow, Max," said Harriet.

I jerked my head away, but in doing so accidentally gulped, and the stone, not used to being treated thusly, decided to gambol it down the hatch. I gulped some more when I realized I was now holding a million-dollar diamond in my tummy!

"Oh, boy," said Brutus. "I think he's going to croak. Look at his face. He's having a seizure or something. Call a doctor!" he yelled. "Max is sick!"

Marge looked up at this, and immediately Odelia came

rushing out of the bathroom. I did feel a little weak, but that was more from the knowledge that I'd just swallowed a diamond, and was now wondering how it would affect my innards.

"Max, are you all right?" asked Marge as she bent down next to me.

"I feel a little faint," I admitted.

"Is your cat all right?" asked the authoress, who seemed momentarily taken aback that Marge's attention, which had been so lavish and unstinted, had suddenly switched to me.

"I think he's not feeling well," said Odelia. "We better take him to a doctor. Max, say something," she urged.

"I just swallowed…" I began.

But then Harriet cried, "He swallowed a bug and now he's dying!"

"Dying!" Dooley cried. "Oh, please, Odelia—quick! Max is dying!"

"I'm so sorry," said Marge, addressing Loretta, who'd been watching the scene with limited interest. "But I think we better take Max to a doctor straight away."

"Oh, absolutely," said Loretta. She didn't seem sorry that we were leaving, and nor would she, since she'd just stolen a precious stone and hadn't had time to hide it yet.

So we left the room, Odelia carrying me in her arms while I still felt a little woozy. But once we were out in the corridor, I finally managed to say, "I swallowed the Pink Lady."

Odelia frowned as she took this in.

"What did he just say?" asked Marge.

We were waiting for the elevator to arrive.

"I think he said he swallowed the Pink Lady," said Odelia.

"He's hallucinating," said Harriet. "It's a common side effect of poisoning by bug."

"I'm not poisoned," I said, a little weakly. "I saw the Pink

Lady lying on the nightstand, took it in my mouth, then accidentally swallowed it and now it's in my tummy."

"Oh, dear," said Odelia as she shared a look of concern with her mom.

"We better get Vena to take a look at you, Max," said the latter.

"Or Dr. Poolittle," Dooley suggested. "He is a miracle worker—the pigeon said so."

"Who's Dr. Poolittle?" asked Marge, puzzled.

"Why, Tex, of course," said Dooley before anyone could stop him. "He's suffering from a midwife crisis and now he wants to be a vet," he explained when Marge merely stared at him. "But don't tell anyone, Marge, cause it's a secret."

"We're going to Vena," said Odelia decidedly.

"Thank you," I said. I hate going to the vet, but if I have to go, I'd much rather go to one who's done her homework, and not an amateur vet who's suffering from a midwife crisis.

"Did you know about this?" Marge asked as we rode the elevator down.

"Um…" said Odelia, trying not to meet her mom's eyes.

"He wants to become a vet? But why?"

"He doesn't like that people show him their moles at Costco's," said Dooley. "And he saved a pigeon's life."

"Moles and pigeons? What is he talking about, honey?"

"I'll tell you all about it in the car," said Odelia.

"Not just moles and pigeons," said Dooley. "He's seeing a badger tonight."

"What's going on!" Marge cried.

28

Unfortunately it would appear that this was not my lucky day. Even though I'd never have admitted it at any other moment in my life, when we discovered the sign hanging on Vena's door that she was on a two-week vacation and to call her replacement in the next town, I actually, and for the first time in my life, wished that Vena had been there!

"We can't wait for an appointment," Odelia said, making one of those executive decisions your pet owner is sometimes obliged to make under these circumstances, and so she and Marge decided that the next best thing to a vet was... Tex!

"Not Dr. Poolittle!" I moaned, for that diamond was really lying heavy on my tummy now. "He's not a real doctor!"

"He actually is a real doctor," said Marge. "In fact he's one of the best doctors I know."

"But he's not a pet doctor!" I lamented.

We were in the car at that point, Odelia having raced across town to Vena's, and now racing back into town to see her dad about a cat. It might have sounded like a joke, but it was no joke to me!

"He's dying, Odelia," said Dooley in a choky voice. "My best friend is dying. Do something! Save him!"

"I'm not dying, Dooley," I assured him. Though it was true that I wasn't exactly feeling at the top of my form.

"That diamond is sharp, Max," said Brutus. "It's sharp and hard and it's probably cutting you all up inside. It's cutting a way through your stomach, then through your liver, through your intestines, and finally it will burrow its way out, through the sheer force of gravity, and by that time you'll die from internal hemorrhaging."

"Why, thank you, Brutus!" I cried. "That's very helpful!"

"Just telling you what you're up against," said a cat who was supposed to be my friend but behaved more like my worst enemy! "Diamonds are used in the mining industry," he continued. "They can cut through the hardest rock. They use them as drill bits, see, since they can cut through almost anything, so they definitely won't have any trouble cutting through your soft tissues, buddy."

"Brutus, maybe you shouldn't say these things to Max," said Harriet. "He's in bad enough shape as it is."

"Yeah, don't say things like that, Brutus!" I cried.

"All right, all right," said the black cat, holding up his paws. "Just thought you'd want to know."

"Oh, Max, you're bleeding!" said Dooley.

I glanced down at the seat of the car, but didn't see a thing. "Bleeding? Where?"

"That's not blood, Dooley," said Harriet. "That's ketchup."

"Are you sure?" said Dooley, and licked at the spot.

"Dooley, how many times do I have to tell you not to lick at strange spots!" I said.

"Oh, Max," he said, giving me a watery smile. "Even now, with one paw in the grave, you still think of me-e-e-e!"

The car pulled to a stop, and we all piled out, though I had the luxury of being carried, since apparently I was now at death's door, with only a few more minutes—or seconds! —to live.

They carried me into the waiting room, then without knocking into the doctor's office, where they found Tex, sipping from a bottle and looking as if he'd been busted in the act of doing something he shouldn't.

"It's just water!" he cried when he met the censorious gazes of his wife and daughter and no less than four cats. "See?" He held up the bottle, and indeed it was Evian—not one of your go-to brands for alcoholics.

"Max swallowed the Pink Lady," said Marge, placing me on the desk in front of the doctor.

"A pink what?" asked Tex.

"The Pink Lady, Tex. The diamond we kept in our bedroom safe?"

"The very large diamond you kept in your bedroom safe," Odelia specified.

"He's accidentally swallowed it, so it's in his stomach, and doing who knows what damage in there."

"And with Vena on holiday…"

"So it's up to you, Tex."

"But…"

"You want to be a vet, right? Well, now's your chance to prove it!"

"You know about that?" asked Tex. He then turned to me. "But I thought Vesta had sworn the cats to secrecy?"

"It's all right, Tex," said Dooley. "I told Marge not to tell anyone."

"You really should know better than to trust cats to keep a secret," said Marge. "They blab. It's what they do!"

"Now save Max's life, Dad," Odelia implored. "Do something!"

I should have felt insulted by Marge's words, but frankly she was right: blabbing is what we do! But then Tex looked me in the eye, and I looked him in the eye, and he smiled. And I don't know why, but at that moment I felt slightly reassured that this man knew what he was doing and that he could help me. After all, he was a doctor, right? He might not be a vet yet, but he knew about anatomy. And since human anatomy probably isn't all that different from that of other mammals, maybe he would be able to save my life from this sharp and pointy diamond!

"Okay, here's what we'll do," said Tex, as he picked me up and carried me over to his examination table. "First we're going to take a picture to see what we're dealing with here."

"A picture?" I asked a little weakly. "You're going to take my picture?"

"Now is not the time to take pictures for your Facebook page, Tex!" Harriet cried.

"I think Tex is referring to an X-ray," Marge explained.

And indeed he was. He hooked me up to some kind of machine hovering over me, and moments later said, "Don't move, Max." So I kept perfectly still while he did his thing.

"The X-ray machine was a big investment," Marge explained to her daughter, "but it's definitely paying off now."

"I only use it for small stuff," said Tex.

"I'm not small stuff, Tex!" I cried, but of course he didn't understand.

"It saves time. Sending a person to a radiologist and then waiting for the results..." He was studying a special kind of laptop now, and finally said, "I see it. It's still in his stomach."

Odelia and Marge crowded around Tex and studied the images. "I seem to remember the Pink Lady is not a sharp-edged stone," said Odelia. "I don't think it'll do any damage."

"Plus, it's round," said Tex. "It should pass through quite easily."

"So what do you suggest?" asked Marge.

"I think you should give him bread and a few spoons of milk. The bread will wrap itself around the diamond and protect the stomach, and the milk will induce a mild case of diarrhea, which will help purge the stone from his system. You'll need to monitor his stool to retrieve the diamond—better wear plastic gloves when you do."

"And if he doesn't pass the diamond?" asked Odelia, stroking me gently.

"If it doesn't pass, it will need to be removed surgically."

"Surgically!" I cried. "What do you mean, surgically?!"

"He means he'll have to operate," Odelia explained.

"He'll have to cut you open like a fish, Max," said Brutus.

"But I don't want to be cut open like a fish!"

"Brutus, don't scare Max," said Harriet.

"I'm just telling him what's going to happen so that he's prepared. It's better that he knows going in. Chances of survival are probably fifty percent," he said. "Though to be honest it can go both ways."

"Brutus!" Harriet snapped.

"All right, all right. Just trying to help."

"Well, stop helping."

"Who's going to perform the procedure?" asked Odelia. "You, Dad?"

"Not me personally, no," said Tex. "I—I'm not qualified to operate on Max." He sighed. "I'm not actually a vet, you see. And if anything went wrong..."

"I know, honey," said Marge, rubbing her husband on the back. "But I still think you did a fine job here." She gave me a smile. "How are you feeling, Max?"

"I guess I'm okay," I said. "As long as Tex won't cut me open like a fish." They'd turned the thick laptop in my direction, and it was a little weird to be able to look inside myself—plenty weird, in fact. And there it was: the Pink Lady. It was just lying there, gently reposing on a bed of stomach, and not doing any cutting or drilling or whatever horrible picture Brutus had conjured up.

"You'll be fine," said Odelia. "You'll poop out the stone and that'll be the end of it."

I glanced up at Tex. "You really are Dr. Poolittle," I said reverently. "Thank you, sir."

After Marge had translated my words to the doctor, he frowned. "Dr. Poolittle? What is he talking about?"

"I came up with that," Dooley said. "It's a cool nickname, don't you think?"

"No, Dooley," said Harriet. "It's a very silly nickname."

"I like it," said Odelia with a grin. "It's very catchy."

"Dr. Poolittle," Tex murmured, rolling the words around his tongue. He didn't seem overly pleased with the moniker. "Is that what Hampton Cove's pet population is calling me?"

"They will now," I said, as I gave the man a mild head bunt.

29

I don't know if you've ever had to wait for a diamond to pass through your gastrointestinal system, but generally speaking it's not an arduous process. You simply let nature take its course and in the meantime you get on with your life. Only in my case it was slightly complicated by the fact that my humans had fed me a few spoons of milk, which causes diarrhea in a lot of cats, me included. And the second complication was the knowledge that people were waiting for me to poop out a million-dollar gem made me slightly anxious—which luckily also aided in the digestive process! And since Odelia wanted me close by so she could monitor my progress—or that of the diamond—I was grounded, which didn't bother me in the slightest. I am, after all, a homebody.

Dooley had decided to keep me company, and was watching me like a hawk, and Brutus and Harriet were in the vicinity, too, having a nice nap underneath the rose bushes in the backyard while Dooley and I enjoyed a lie-down on the smooth lawn. And so the long day wore on, with Odelia popping her head out of the upstairs window from time to time to check on me, and me feeling like a sick pet and taking it easy, even though technically I wasn't sick—just silly enough to swallow a priceless gem!

"I think we should take it easy, Max," said Dooley when I got up to stretch. "We don't want to exert ourselves."

"I'm fine, Dooley," I said. "I'm not actually sick, just inconvenienced."

"We don't look fine, Max. We look… constipated."

I grimaced. It was true that in spite of Tex's ministrations nothing was happening, if you know what I mean. "Maybe milk isn't strong enough. Maybe I need an actual laxative."

"A laxative? You mean something that will make us poop?"

"Yes, Dooley. That's what a laxative is. It makes you go poop. And what's with all the 'we' stuff? I'm the one with the diamond up his… keister."

He thought about this for a moment. "Maybe grass?" he suggested. "Grass might get things moving down… there." He vaguely gestured to my lower strata.

"Trouble, boys?" asked Brutus, who'd come wandering up, followed by Harriet.

"Nothing I can't handle, Brutus," I said, perhaps a little curtly. Frankly I could do without the black cat's advice.

"We can't poop," announced Dooley, the inveterate blabbermouth. "And so we're thinking about eating some grass."

"We?" asked Harriet. "Did you swallow a diamond, too?"

But Brutus was laughing. "You want to eat grass? Like a cow? That's hilarious!"

"Not like a cow, Brutus," I said. "It's a generally known fact that cats eat grass to help with their digestion."

"Wanna know what I think?" said Brutus as he regarded me thoughtfully.

"No, Brutus, I do not want to know what you think."

"I think that diamond is stuck down there. And now the

whole process is blocked." When I produced a light laugh at this, he continued, "I'm not trying to be funny, Max. When an object as large as that diamond gets stuck in your intestine, whether it be the small intestine or the large, it creates a blockage that could be fatal if not immediately remedied."

"Fatal!" Dooley cried, in a panic all over again.

"Nothing is stuck, Brutus," I assured him. "It just takes time. It's only been, what, two hours? And the whole process takes seven to twelve hours." Tex had told me this, and I believed him.

"Do you want to take that chance?" Brutus said, cocking an eyebrow at me. "Cats have died from this, buddy. And as your good friend I'm telling you that you should go and see a doctor. Pronto."

"Oh, God," said Harriet, rolling her eyes. "Not again."

"Odeliaaaa!" Dooley was already screaming. "Odeliaaaaaaaaaaaa!"

Odelia's head popped out of the bedroom window so fast she hit it against the top of the frame. "Ouch. What's wrong?"

"The diamond is stuck in Max's butt and he needs to see the doctor NOW!" Dooley screamed. "Or he will DIEEEEEEEE!"

"Wait, I'm coming down," said Odelia. And indeed moments later she joined us on the lawn. "What's all this about the diamond being stuck?"

"Max hasn't pooped yet," Brutus explained, "so that diamond is probably stopping up his whole system, and that is a very dangerous situation, and one that should be handled ASAP."

"Max?" Asked Odelia, directing a concerned look in my direction. "Are you in pain right now? Do you feel as if something's blocked down there?"

"I feel fine!" I assured everyone. "So stop worrying. The doctor said this could take hours."

"Have you pooped yet?" asked Brutus. "It's a simple question."

"No, I haven't."

"I rest my case," said the butch cat.

"Mh," said Odelia, then took out her phone, and moments later was consulting with her dad. When she hung up, she had a look of concern on her face, a look I certainly didn't like to see there! "He says to come in. He'll take another X-ray to see how far the diamond has progressed through your system."

I produced a sound of disappointment. I hate going to the doctor, and now I had to go twice in one day? But what could I do? Dr. Poolittle had spoken, and so I had to do what he said. And so moments later we all piled in the car again, and were on our way into town.

"Mh," said Tex as he studied the screen. "I don't like what I'm seeing, honey."

"Do you think the diamond is blocked?" asked Odelia, nervous now.

"There is some progress, but according to my calculations it should have been further along at this point. And the fact that he hasn't had a bowel movement is worrying me."

"Don't say these things, Dr. Poolittle," I lamented. "Now you've got me worried, too!"

"Maybe you could use a plunger?" Brutus suggested. "It works miracles on stopped-up drains and toilets, or so I've been told."

"Nobody is using a plunger on me!" I yelled.

"Relax, buddy," said Brutus with a grin. "Just kidding."

"Oh, snuggle bear," said Harriet. "Now is not the time for jokes."

"I was just trying to lighten the mood, snow bunny."

Harriet giggled. "I actually thought it was pretty funny."

"So what do you suggest, Dad?" asked Odelia.

Tex lowered his head to examine my butt more closely. "Well, I would suggest that…"

And I would have listened with distinct interest to the doctor's suggestions, but just at that moment I felt a sudden urge taking control over me—a powerful spasm in my lower regions, if you see what I mean—and moments later there was a minor explosion, and when all was said and done, I'd done my business right there on Tex's nice exam table. It felt good, I can tell you—immensely good. As if I'd just passed a brick!

"Max! You did it!" Dooley cried.

"Good boy," said Odelia, patting me on the head.

"Way to go, Max!" said Harriet.

"And you didn't even need a plunger," said Brutus with a big grin.

But then Tex slowly rose from behind me, and we all watched as remnants of my digestive process dribbled off his face. It was in his eyes, his nose, his hair, even his mouth, for he'd just been saying something.

"Oh, Dad!" said Odelia with a horrified laugh. "You should see yourself!"

"He got the full load," Brutus said reverently. "The whole enchilada."

Odelia handed the doctor a wet wipe and as he glanced down at himself and his nice shiny exam table, a sort of howl escaped his lips. "My table!" he cried. "My office!"

"Oh, don't be such a baby, Dad," said Odelia. "This is all part and parcel of being a vet. Now let's find that diamond!"

It didn't take her long to find the Pink Lady, and I have to say the atmosphere was jubilant—a tough job well done!

The only one who didn't seem to share in the revels was Tex. He'd cleaned himself up at this point, but still didn't look happy about the whole business.

"What's wrong, Dad?" asked Odelia finally.

"I don't think I'm cut out for this," the good doctor confessed.

"Cut out for what?"

"This… animal!" he cried, gesturing to me and to his table, which still bore witness of recent events.

"Max is not an animal, Dad," said Odelia sternly. "Max is family."

"But look at what he did to my nice table! It smells!"

"So you clean it. Big deal. Haven't you ever dealt with this kind of thing before?"

"If you're asking me if a patient ever pooped on my face—no, as a matter of fact they haven't."

"Well, if you're going to be a vet you can't afford to be squeamish, Dad. So get a grip, will you?"

"I can't do this," said Tex, shaking his head.

"If you think this is bad, try pulling a calf from a cow with your bare hands," said Odelia.

Tex gulped at the picture Odelia's words conjured up. "I guess I had a more romantic view of the life of a vet. Healing sick birds and dealing with roupy chickens. Maybe a colicky collie."

"You know what you should do?" said Harriet. "You should ask Vena if you can assist her for a couple of days at the practice. Then you'll see what it's really like to be a vet. And if you still like it, then you can decide."

Odelia dutifully translated Harriet's words for the doctor, and Tex nodded. "She's right—you're right. You're all absolutely right!"

"I feel all right," I intimated, still on cloud nine after my accomplishment. I don't know if you've ever noticed, but when cats have had a good poo, they feel on top of the world, and that's how I felt right now.

"Anyway, we can discuss your future as a vet tonight," said Odelia. "Right now we need to take this diamond to Uncle

Alec, and also tell him to arrest Loretta Gray for trying to steal it."

"Maybe you should hold off on that," I said. I'd been doing some thinking while I was lying in that backyard waiting for a certain stone to pop from a certain orifice, and I'd come to the conclusion that the situation wasn't as clear-cut as it looked.

"What do you mean?" said Odelia with a frown.

So I proceeded to lay out my most recent brainstorm to the small gathering—except for Tex, who'd returned to the bathroom, presumably to wash his face with bleach.

30

Vesta was at the General Store doing some last-minute shopping when she saw Scarlett pass by the store, hand in hand with none other than… Johnny Carew. After she'd sufficiently recovered from the shock, she walked out, her bag of groceries in her hand, and accosted her friend. "Scarlett, why don't you pick up your phone?"

"Oh, did you call me?" asked Scarlett, looking radiant and clearly enamored with this big lug.

"Several times."

"Well, I've been busy," said Scarlett with a cheeky grin.

"And I can see who you've been busy with," said Vesta, directing a curious look at Johnny.

"Hi, Mrs. Muffin," said the former criminal. "Scarlett and I are in love."

"Of course you are," said Vesta.

"Ever since we met I've had flies in the pit of my stomach," said Johnny. "I even told Jerry. 'Jer,' I said, 'I have flies in the pit of my stomach,' I said. And you know what he said?"

"I have no idea."

"He said I'm crazy, and he's right, I am crazy—crazy about this lady!"

He placed a large arm around Scarlett's shoulders, and the latter gave Vesta a wink, which Vesta returned.

"So we're still on for the neighborhood watch?" asked Vesta.

"Absolutely."

"What watch?" asked Johnny.

"Oh, just a little project Vesta and I got going," said Scarlett, patting the big man's chest. "Nothing for you to worry about."

And as they walked off, Johnny said, "I wasn't lying, Scarlett. I really do feel flies in the pit of my stomach."

"Are you sure it's not butterflies, Johnny?" asked Scarlett.

"Pretty sure it's flies, Scarlett."

"All right, honey. If you say it's flies, it's flies."

Shaking her head, Vesta walked on, a small smile lifting the corners of her lips. Scarlett and her men. She gave Johnny a week—two weeks, tops.

"Vesta, wait up!" suddenly a voice rang out behind her. She frowned and turned, and saw that Wilbur Vickery wanted a word.

"Wilbur?"

"I need your advice," said the store owner as he licked his lips. Judging from the pink-colored crumbs, he'd been eating a glazed donut. "I met this woman, see?"

"You met a woman?"

"Uh-huh. Her name is Loretta Gray and she's a famous writer or something. So we went out twice, but since our last date she won't return my calls or my messages and she's blocked me on Facebook. What do you think that means?"

Vesta rolled her eyes. "What do you think it means, Wilbur?"

"That there won't be a third date?"

"Bingo! See? You didn't need my advice after all."

"But there was definitely chemistry between us. I could tell."

"Don't tell me. Flies in the pit of your stomach?"

"Well, no," he said, looking confused. Wilbur's face was not one of your handsome faces. He had skin like the surface of the moon, and his teeth had seen better days—a couple of decades ago. But what he lacked in outward appearance, he made up for in sheer tenacity when pursuing the object of his affection.

"How many messages did you send this lady?"

"Oh, hundreds, probably?"

"That's your mistake right there, Wilbur. No woman likes to be harassed."

"But I thought women liked to be pursued?"

"There's a fine line between being pursued and being harassed, and from what you just told me you're on the wrong side of it. So back off already, will you, before she calls the cops on you for stalking."

"You think?"

"Of course." He was staring at her like a lost puppy now, and she took pity on the guy. "Look, if you want I'll talk to the woman. Is she local?"

"She's staying at the Star hotel. Room two-fourteen. I've thought about serenading her but her window is at the back. And I've left messages at the desk but no dice."

"Okay, I'll go over there right now and see what's going on. But don't get your hopes up, buddy."

"Oh, thank you, Vesta. Thank you, thank you, thank you."

"Don't thank me yet, Casanova. She'll probably tell me to take a hike, and if she does, I can't say I blame her."

31

The meeting had been arranged and took place in the suite of the Star hotel. Present were four cats, Marge, Odelia and Chase, and two people I'd never met before: the Sheikh was there, of course, and a guy named Sharif Maroun, whose job description wasn't exactly clear to me but who I assumed was some kind of advisor. There were also plenty of security people hovering around, but upon a word from the Sheikh they'd left the suite and now it was just us and the ruler of Khemed. I had expected at least a couple of the man's wives to be present, but apparently they had better things to do. The only woman present, apart from Marge and Odelia, was in fact Loretta Gray, though it was obvious from her expression that she wasn't exactly happy to be there.

"So you have managed to retrieve the Pink Lady?" said Sheikh Bab El Ghat. "That is very good news indeed, Mrs. Poole."

He glanced between Odelia and Marge, since they had both nodded in acknowledgment.

"I'm Mrs. Poole since my husband is Mr. Poole," Marge

explained. "And my daughter is Mrs. Poole since her dad is my husband."

"Oh, this is ridiculous," said Odelia. "Just call me Mrs. Kingsley, because my husband is Mr. Kingsley."

Chase, who was standing next to her, looked up in surprise, and a happy smile flitted across his face, then disappeared again, replaced by his standard cop-on-duty expression.

The Sheikh, who was younger than I thought, smiled and extended his hands. "Well, when can I feast my eyes on this precious stone? Or do you want to keep me in suspense?"

"Here she is," said Marge, and handed the stone to the Sheikh. She'd placed it back in its box, and when the Sheikh opened the box, he blinked at the stone's sheer splendor.

"Oh, my," he said. "This certainly is a gorgeous specimen, isn't it, Sharif?"

He held it up so his advisor could take a peek, but the man didn't look particularly impressed.

"Very nice," were his only words, spoken without much excitement.

"I thought this stone was lost forever, and now all of a sudden here it is," said the Sheikh as he stared at the diamond, mesmerized.

"It was a lucky coincidence that it was found on our shores, your highness," Odelia agreed.

"Please, just call me Bab," said the young Sheikh with a wave of the hand. He was a handsome ruler, with slicked-back dark hair and eyes the color of amber. He was dressed in designer jeans, a pink polo shirt and sneakers, unlike his advisor Sharif, who was dressed in a gray suit and sporting sunglasses, even though we were indoors. They both looked pretty hip and cool, I thought.

"So what are you going to do with the stone... Bab?" asked Chase.

"I think I'll put it on display in our national museum," said the Sheikh with a little nod of satisfaction as he clicked the jewel box closed and pocketed it.

"Sir?" said Sharif.

"Yes, I don't want to lock it up in a vault. I want the people of Khemed to be able to admire its beauty. So the museum is the best place."

"You're not going to give it to one of your wives?" asked Marge.

"One of my wives?" said the Sheikh with a curt laugh. "As far as I'm aware I only have one wife."

"Oh, I just assumed…"

"One of our traditions I decided to dispense with," the Sheikh explained. "And now please tell me all about the Pink Lady, and how it ended up in Hampton Cove of all places."

"I think the person best placed to tell you that story," said Odelia, "is this lady over here. Loretta? Will you do the honors?"

"Loretta wrote a very interesting book about the Pink Lady and its history," Marge explained. "Which is why we asked her to be present when we handed you the diamond."

Loretta looked a little uncomfortable as she took a short curtsy, then said, "Your highness… Bab."

"So you wrote a book about the Pink Lady? I haven't read it yet, but now I can't wait."

"I think you'll find it very interesting," said Marge. "It's based on a real story."

Loretta gave Marge an icy glance. "Marge is flattering me. I'm afraid the book is a figment of my imagination. Inspired by the true story of the Pink Lady, but only in a very limited way."

"Oh," said the Sheikh, slightly disappointed, then turned to Marge, clearly expecting an explanation.

"Loretta looks very uncomfortable, Max," said Dooley.

"Yes, she does," I agreed.

When we'd arrived at the hotel, and had knocked on Loretta's door for the second time that day, she'd been most surprised to see us. She also looked very flustered, presumably because she'd been looking everywhere for that diamond that had gone missing. Which is probably also why she gave us a look of extreme suspicion. So when Odelia had invited her to be present at the official handing over of the famous diamond to its rightful owner, her eyes had gone wide, but since she couldn't very well come out and say that she had taken the stone, and especially with Chase right there, she reluctantly decided to play along, no doubt all the while wondering how we'd managed to take the stone, and why she hadn't been arrested yet.

"You're being too modest, Loretta," said Marge now. "The story of the Pink Lady did a lot more than inspire you, didn't it? In fact I think it's safe to say that you lived part of that story yourself."

Loretta's eyes were blazing, as she looked from Odelia to Marge, clearly wondering what they were playing at.

"I don't understand," said the young Sheikh. "You *lived* part of the story?"

"Mrs. Poole is speaking figuratively," said Loretta. "Writers live in their imagination, and my imagination is what inspired me, loosely based on an article I read about the Pink Lady."

"That's not what I meant and you know it," said Marge.

Loretta, who clearly wanted to be anywhere but there, plastered a polite smile on her face. "I'm sure I don't know *what* you mean, Marge."

"And I think that you do."

The Sheikh had followed the back and forth with marked interest, like a spectator at a tennis match. "What's going on? Can anyone explain? You, Mrs. Kingsley?"

"What's going on here is that the real story of the Pink Lady has been shrouded in mystery for far too long, Bab. And I think that the time has come to reveal the truth."

"The truth? The truth about what, exactly?"

"For that we have to go back thirty-five years, to an auspicious moment in your father's life—and that of Laura Burns, his ninety-ninth bride and the recipient of the Pink Lady."

"Yes, Laura Burns," said the Sheikh. "She died shortly after giving birth to a child, then that child also died. A very sad day for my father, and for the people of my country."

"Laura died," said Marge," but her daughter didn't. Instead she was smuggled out of the country the day her mother died, along with the Pink Lady."

The young Sheikh frowned. "What are you talking about? Smuggled out of the country? By who?"

"I think perhaps Loretta is best placed to tell you all about it," said Odelia.

"Loretta? Why?"

"Because her real name is Bab El Ahs, your highness. And she's your sister."

32

The moment Odelia had uttered these words, a couple of things happened: the Sheikh's jaw dropped, Sharif's head jerked round to direct an astonished look at Loretta, and the latter rushed out the door. Unfortunately for her, just at that moment Gran tried to walk in, and as a consequence the two ladies collided.

"Oh, there you all are," said Gran as she tried to glance past Loretta, who tried to get past Gran. "I'm looking for Loretta Gray, and the two heavies watching the door told me she's in here."

"That's Loretta," I said, pointing to the author who was still trying to get past Gran but was failing to do so. Gran is a hard person to dislodge if she doesn't want to be dislodged, which she usually doesn't.

"Oh, hi there," said Gran, and held out her hand for Loretta to shake. "I'm a friend of Wilbur Vickery's, and he's asked me to have a little chat. Turns out you had a bad reaction to your second date with him—don't worry, it happens all the time—in fact it happened on my first date with him—and now he's worried that he said something wrong, which, knowing him, he did, and wants to see if there's anything he can do to fix it, which I'm sure he can't, but anyway, just thought I'd look in on you and see if there's any lasting damage, if you know what I mean." But then she must have noticed that Loretta was on the verge of tears, and her face fell. "Oh, dear. He's done it again, hasn't he? Wilbur can be a boor, but deep down he's all right, you know. Harmless, I mean."

"It's not that," said Loretta, then glanced back. And when her eyes met the Sheikh's, she produced a faint smile. "I guess I owe you an explanation, don't I?"

"Yes, I guess you do," said the Sheikh, still looking flabbergasted.

At this point Gran must have come to the conclusion that something entirely different was going on, so she frowned and said, "What's going on?"

"Come in, Gran, and close the door," said Odelia, and then Loretta returned on her steps, Gran did as she was told, and we all listened as the author of The Sheikh's Passion told her story.

"Thirty-five years ago my mother realized that she was in trouble," Loretta began. We'd all accepted the Sheikh's invitation to take a seat in the suite's salon, and had made ourselves comfortable. Tea had been served, and sweet cookies, and Marge had taken out a tissue, just in case Loretta's story was as touching as the book she'd read.

"I think I know the kind of trouble you mean," said Gran as she nibbled from a cookie. "She met a nice boy and got herself pregnant, huh?"

"More or less," said Loretta.

"Just let the woman talk, Ma," said Marge, who sat poised on her chair as if at a library reading.

"My mother had married Sheikh Bab El Ehr out of love, and at first things between them were great. But the trouble began soon after their wedding ceremony. You see, my mother had been raised in the traditions of the West, and she wasn't used to the way things were done in Khemed, even though she'd lived there most of her life, except the years she spent in New York. Her parents had raised her a free spirit, and were very much surprised when she fell in love with the Sheikh and accepted his proposal. They warned her that this might not be a good idea. That an entire structure had been put in place around the Sheikh that would make it impossible for her to live the kind of life she wanted to live. But she was young and in love, and the Sheikh made her all kinds of promises, so she threw caution and the advice of her parents to the wind and decided to marry anyway. The Sheikh had told her before they married that he'd instigate a process of modernization, and that he'd send his other wives back to their families and she would be his only wife. He'd promised her they'd have children, and they'd be the only heirs to the throne. He'd also given her the Pink Lady as a token of his love and affection, and said it was hers to keep, whatever happened, even though the stone had been part of the country's set of royal jewels until then."

"I like the story, Max," said Dooley. "It's almost like a novel, isn't it?"

"It is," I said. "Though unlike a novel, it actually happened."

"Which makes it even better," he said. Dooley is a big fan of soap operas, and there was a touch of the outlandish about the story Loretta was telling. No wonder Gran was also listening with rapt attention, as she, too, is a soap aficionado.

"So shortly before their one-year wedding anniversary, things came to a head. By this time it had become clear to my mother that her husband had no intention of keeping the promises he made. Those ninety-eight other wives were still very much established at the palace, and weren't going anywhere. Quite the contrary, in fact. The palace was abuzz with rumors of a coup mother wanted to stage against the Sheikh, rumors designed to drive a wedge between the couple. The Sheikh spent less and less time in my mother's quarters, and slept less and less in the spousal bed, opting to spend his nights with his other wives, in other parts of the palace, where she wasn't even allowed to go. She was slowly being sidelined, and that wasn't the life she'd chosen for herself, or the baby she was carrying. Worse, her passport had been taken away by palace officials, and she'd been forbidden to leave, allegedly for her own safety, but it was clear she was now a prisoner rather than the person in charge of the royal household. She wasn't even allowed to talk to her parents anymore, who'd returned to the States, or her old friends, and things looked more and more dire."

"Oh, dear," said Marge, clasping a hand to her face. "This is the part of the book I haven't read yet," she explained when all eyes turned to her. "But please go on."

"Yes, please go on," said the Sheikh, who looked stunned by this story—clearly a story nobody had ever told him.

"So the day my mother was supposed to give birth finally arrived, and word had reached her ears that the other wives had arranged for her baby to be smothered in its cradle."

"What?!" Marge cried, shooting upright. "I'm sorry," she murmured, settling down again. "Don't mind me."

"They felt that a new heir would jeopardize their position to such an extent it was better to get rid of the child altogether. So mother was desperate, especially since she had no one she could turn to—no one who could help. But then salvation came in the form of two men who worked for a large hydroelectric project. Their names were Craig Bantam and Kenneth Cesseki and they were both Americans. She'd seen them walking in the palace garden with the Sheikh, and so one day she managed to sneak a message to one of the men, Craig, and arranged to meet him in secret in the garden, and explained her predicament. Craig, who must have had a noble heart, promised her he'd do what he could, and so she met him in secret several times more, and gradually a plan was hatched to help her escape the palace, along with the baby, so no harm could be done to either mother or child."

"And you're saying that my father was complicit in all of this?" asked the Sheikh, who still looked stunned.

"I don't know if he was complicit, or if he simply didn't want to know what was going on, but he certainly didn't listen to my mother, and didn't arrange for her to be taken to safety, or punish the people conspiring against her," said Loretta, who'd folded her hands in her lap, and was telling her story serenely, clearly glad to finally get it out. "So my mother had given birth, and had watched my cradle day and night, to prevent anything happening to me, and the day finally arrived that Craig and Kenneth were to smuggle my mother out of the palace, along with me, but something went wrong. Both men were arrested and subsequently deported. Also, my mother had become violently ill during the night, and had to be taken to the hospital. She died later that day."

"I'm so sorry," said Odelia.

"But Craig and Kenneth had arranged for a palace servant, one of the rare ones loyal to my mother, to set the plan in motion regardless of what happened to its protagonists. And this brave servant managed to smuggle me out of the palace, and drove me out of the country, across the border into Khamsin, and from there I was flown to safety in America, where Craig proceeded to hand me to my grandmother and grandfather. They were devastated to learn of the death of their only daughter, but happy to be able to take care of me. And they raised me," she said simply.

"And told you the story of what happened," Odelia supplied.

Loretta nodded. "They told me on my eighteenth birthday. Until that moment I had no idea who my mother was, or even what had actually happened to her. My grandparents had always told me they were my parents, until they decided the time had come to tell me the truth."

"But… what happened to the Pink Lady?" asked Gran.

"My mother, before she became ill, had fastened the ring to my diaper," said Loretta, "so when Craig's contact person at the palace smuggled me out, unbeknownst to her she also smuggled out the diamond. It was actually my grandmother who discovered the stone when she changed my diaper for the first time, after I'd arrived in New York. And since it was such a famous diamond, they were at a loss what to do with it. So it was decided that Craig would keep it safe until I'd come of age. Unfortunately Craig died before he could tell my grandparents where he'd hidden the diamond, and so it stayed in his safe at the bank all these years until two crooks burgled the bank and this whole rigmarole with the stone began."

"Which is why you decided to take possession of it," said Odelia.

"It is rightfully mine," said Loretta with a touch of defiance. "It belonged to my mother, and she intended for me to have it. It's the only thing of hers I have." She now regarded the Sheikh sternly. "It certainly doesn't belong to you, sir, since it was by your father's hand, or one of his wives, that my mother died."

The Sheikh blinked at this, and a slight flush of crimson crept up his cheeks. "Are you accusing my father of murder?"

"Craig told my parents that rumor had it that my mother was poisoned," said Loretta, "and who else than a person with access to her could have done that?"

"Look, this is all ancient history now," said Sharif, stirring for the first time. "And frankly I think you should ask yourself, sir, why this person suddenly comes up with this story so many years after the fact?"

"I didn't 'come up' with the story," said Loretta. "This is the story as it happened."

But the Sheikh nodded thoughtfully. "Go on, Sharif."

"I think," said Sharif, "that Miss Gray here is not your father's daughter, sir, but a fraud and a con artist. And the only reason she's telling this preposterous story is to get her hands on the diamond."

"There's an easy way to decide whether Loretta is telling the truth or not," said Odelia. "Do a DNA test. If it's positive, you'll know that she's your half-sister, Bab."

"Oh, this is simply ridiculous," said Sharif. "Of course she's not your sister, sir. Please don't listen to these people."

"No, but Mrs. Kingsley is right, Sharif. A DNA test won't take long, and it will decide this matter one way or another."

"I strongly advise you not to subject yourself to a test," said Sharif emphatically. "It can only lead to rumor and innuendo. The mere fact that you agreed to a test would cause people to give credence to this woman's words. They'll think that where there's smoke, there must be fire. Miss Gray will be able to feast on these rumors for years, appear on talk shows, get book deals, start a podcast..."

"Look, I don't care whether you believe me or not," said Loretta. "All I want is the Pink Lady. It's the only memory of my mother I have, and she wanted me to have it."

"The Pink Lady wasn't your mother's to give," said the Sheikh. "It belongs to the people of Khemed. Your mother had no right to give it to these American operatives."

"Exactly right, sir," said Sharif, gloating slightly. "Now let's end this matter once and for all and return home. Our mission was to retrieve the stone, and we have accomplished that, so let's not waste any more time with this adventuress."

The Sheikh regarded Loretta for a moment, then said, "No, I want to get to the bottom of this. I want to do the DNA test."

"But, sir!"

"It's done, Sharif," said the Sheikh, and his tone brooked no contest.

"Very well, sir," said Sharif, who clearly knew when he had been overruled. "I'll arrange it."

Our audience with the Sheikh was at an end, and so we all filed out of the suite, Loretta to return to her own room, and the rest of us to go home. But before we left, Loretta had something to say. "I owe you an apology, Marge," she said as we stood in the hallway waiting for the elevator to take us down. "I lied to you about who I was, and about the reasons for me to write the book."

"And I want to apologize to you, Loretta," said Marge, "for the subterfuge. I followed you after you received the Pink Lady from that insurance man and then made up an excuse to see you and keep you busy while my daughter searched around for the diamond."

Loretta smiled. "I knew it must have been you who took it. At first I thought it was the cleaner, since she came in shortly before you arrived, and I blamed myself for not hiding it better. But I didn't have time, and besides, I didn't think anyone would suspect me of taking the stone."

"That was very clever of you, arranging things with Dwayne Late and Oscar Godish," said Odelia.

"Well, I had to do something. After I discovered the stone had been found, I wanted to get my hands on it before the Sheikh and his cronies did." She sounded bitter all of a sudden.

"You really think your father had your mother killed?" asked Chase.

"Yes, I do. Craig thought so, too. She was in excellent health, and then all of a sudden within the space of a few hours she died? And just before she had arranged to escape the palace? Craig was absolutely certain she'd been poisoned, and most probably by my father or one of the other wives."

"I talked to Kenneth, and he told me a different story," said Odelia. "He said they met your mother, and were immediately kicked out of the country afterward."

Loretta smiled. "He told me you'd sent him a message through Skype and wanted to talk. He wanted to know what to tell you, so we made some alterations to the story."

"So what about the book?" asked Marge.

"What about the book?"

"What you just told us in there is all in the book, right? So what was the point of hiding the truth from Odelia?"

Loretta shook her head. "Only parts of what actually happened are in the book—mostly the Sheikh and my mother's romance and wedding. I decided that the book had to have a happy end, so the character in the book lives happily ever after with her sheikh, and so does their baby girl."

"Aww," said Gran.

"So why write it?" asked Marge

"After my grandparents told me the real story of who I was, I found myself writing it all down, and before I knew it I'd written the beginning of a book. I guess I wanted to bring my mother's story into the world. Until that point no one had even an inkling of what had happened to her, and I felt that was so unfair. I wanted people to know that she had existed, and what a lovely, wonderful person she had been. I also wrote it to feel closer to her—to build a connection to this person I'd never known, but who was so brave and who'd saved my life."

"By smuggling you out of the country."

"My grandparents actually had to stop me from telling the full story. They didn't want me to put myself in harm's way. The Sheikh has agents everywhere, through Khemed's embassies. He does a lot of business here, and they didn't want me to draw a target on my back. They lost a daughter—they didn't want to lose a granddaughter, too. So that's why the book only tells half the story."

"I guess now your cover is blown," said Odelia.

"I know. I should have known that going after the Pink Lady would get me into trouble."

"How did you persuade Late and Godish to hand the diamond to you?" asked Chase.

Loretta smiled. "Money, Detective. My grandparents are very affluent people, and when they saw how determined I was to get that diamond, they offered me their support."

"How much?"

"Ten percent of what the Pink Lady would fetch at auction."

Chase whistled through his teeth. "They cleaned up."

But then the elevator finally arrived, and we rode down a couple of floors, then Loretta got out. And as the elevator door closed, and she gave us a small wave, suddenly I had a premonition, and not a good one either.

"You guys," I said. "I think maybe we should do something to protect Loretta."

"You think she might be in danger?" asked Odelia.

"What is he saying?" asked Chase.

"He's saying that he thinks Loretta needs protection."

Chase's expression hardened. "Yeah, he's probably right. I don't trust that Sheikh further than I can throw him. He's got crook written all over him. Just like his dad."

"We better go back up," said Marge as she punched the elevator button feverishly. But elevators have a mind of their own, and this one inexorably led us down, and only when we'd reached the lobby did it relinquish the reins of its functionality. And so moments later we were zooming back up again. Only when we arrived on Loretta's floor, she was gone, and when we made our way over to her room, and knocked, there was no answer.

Yikes!

33

But then I put my ear to the door in a move born from desperation, and thought I heard a noise.

"She's in there, all right," I said.

"She's in there," said Odelia.

Chase knocked on the door again, and shouted, "Loretta? Are you all right? Loretta?"

"Loretta, open the door, it's us," said Marge, adding her voice to the chorus.

"Oh, don't just stand there," said Gran finally, when no answer was forthcoming. "Mr. Kingsley, tear down this door!"

Chase hesitated for a moment, but only for a moment, then a look of resolution came into his eyes, and he put his mighty shoulder against the door and gave it a powerful shove. When we all tumbled into the room, the sight that met our eyes was one to behold: there Loretta was, on the bed, with Sharif Maroun on top of her, his hands tightly wrapped around her throat, clearly not with the best intentions in mind!

A certain amount of screaming followed, but once again

it was Chase who proved himself the man of action, by pouncing on the Sheikh's advisor and bodily dragging him off the unfortunate novelist, and in doing so saving the woman's life.

"She's purple, Max," said Dooley as he studied the novelist's face. "Why is she purple?"

"Humans turn purple when they're being strangled," I explained.

"It's not a good sign," Brutus said. "It means they're almost dead."

"No, first they turn red, then purple, and finally when they're dead they turn completely white," said Harriet.

Cats, of course, always keep the same color, or at least on the surface. What we look like underneath our nice fur is our secret and one we will never tell!

"Loretta!" Marge cried, and in two great strides had reached the woman and was offering her support.

"We better get a doctor in here," said Odelia with concern.

"No doctor necessary," said Loretta, already recovering. "But a cop would come in handy right about now. That man tried to kill me!" she said, pointing an accusing finger at Sharif.

"I know, we saw it," Gran said. "And as luck would have it, Chase here is a cop. Please do the honors, Chase."

"You can't arrest me," said Sharif, who was sweating from the exertion, and panting, too. "I have diplomatic immunity, so you can't touch me."

"We'll see about that," said Marge.

"No, he's probably right," said Chase. "If he's got diplomatic immunity he'll walk."

"So he can just try to murder Loretta and get away with it?" Marge cried. "No way!"

"Let's get your uncle in here," Chase suggested to Odelia, "and let him decide."

"I think it's pretty clear now," said Odelia, "that your mother was killed, Loretta, and I think we know who did the killing."

All eyes turned to Sharif, and when moments later suddenly the Sheikh walked in, carrying a bouquet of flowers, and took in the scene, he said, in a surprised voice, "What's going on?"

"Your guy just tried to kill me," said Loretta, still a little hoarse.

"What?!"

"It's true, we all saw it," said Marge.

The Sheikh turned to his advisor. "Have you lost your mind?"

"She's a threat to you, sir," said Sharif, who must have felt safe in the knowledge that whatever he said, nobody could touch him. "She was going to tell the whole story about what happened to her mother, and about the history of the Pink Lady. We don't need that kind of attention, especially now that we're about to sign a number of very lucrative business deals in this country."

"I don't believe this," said the Sheikh. "You're admitting that you tried to kill… my sister?"

"Merely eliminating an obstacle, sir," said Sharif as he adjusted his costume and smoothed his hair, which had become ruffled in the scuffle.

"The same way you removed an obstacle when you killed her mother thirty-five years ago?" asked Odelia.

Sharif shrugged. "The lady was a nuisance. Something had to be done. She was going to flee the palace and tell the world what a backward nation we were, and what a terrible person the Sheikh was. So I handled her."

"Handled her!" the Sheikh roared. "So you admit you murdered my father's wife?"

"I didn't personally kill her, sir. I merely supplied the materials, and organized the operation."

"And what about my father? Did he order this?" asked the Sheikh.

"Oh, no, sir. I didn't see the need to inform him."

"But you did whisper in the man's ear that he should distance himself from his wife, didn't you?" asked Marge.

"Well, of course. The woman was threatening to destroy a tradition we spent centuries building. She wanted to abolish polygyny, the right of a man to marry multiple wives, and make sweeping changes, not just at the palace, but in society as a whole. She was a dangerous element and had to be isolated, then eliminated, for the greater good and to safeguard our traditions and way of life."

"I don't believe this," said the Sheikh, upsetting his own very nice hair by dragging a hand through it. "So you murdered my father's wife, and now you tried to murder her daughter, my sister."

"Murder is such a loaded term, sir," said Sharif. "I like to think of it as providing a permanent solution to a difficult problem."

"Looks like this isn't the first time you've done this," Chase grunted, as he clearly had to restrain himself from giving the fellow a good thrashing.

"Look, I'm very sorry," said the Sheikh. "If I'd known…" He turned to Loretta. "Are you all right?"

"I'll live," croaked Loretta, touching her throat, where we could clearly see Sharif's fingers imprinted on her skin.

"This is just terrible. First off, I want you to arrest this man."

"Sir!" said Sharif.

"I can't," said Chase. "He's got diplomatic immunity, so we can't touch him."

"Fine. I'll deal with him myself," said the Sheikh. "And as

far as you are concerned, I think I owe you all a large debt of gratitude. A debt of gratitude so big I don't even know where to begin." He offered Loretta a toothy smile—the man had a great dentist. "It took thirty-five years for us to meet, but now that I found you—or you found me—I don't want to have this unexpected connection severed again. Please take me to meet your grandparents, so I can personally tell them what a fine job they did raising you, and to offer my sincere apologies for this man's atrocities."

"I merely did what was best for the country," said Sharif stiffly.

"Well, you'll be able to spend the rest of your life contemplating your crimes… in prison," said the Sheikh. And when two burly guards finally materialized in the room, he said, "Please take this man into custody. He's to be deported back to Khemed at once and tried for his crimes."

And as Sharif was led away, the Sheikh shook his head. "What a terrible, terrible waste. I've vowed to change the way things are done in my country, and this is a good moment to start. By getting rid of the old regime, and instituting some sweeping changes."

"Better watch out," said Chase. "Or else they'll try to strangle you, too."

"Thank you for the warning, Mr. Kingsley. I'll take the necessary precautions." He regarded his sister's bruises with a look of anger mixed with sadness. "I better take you to see my doctor."

"You have a doctor?" Loretta croaked.

"Are you kidding? I never travel without my personal physician. One of the perks of being sheikh."

We watched brother and sister leave, and just as they walked out, a man walked in. "Who asked for a hairdresser?" he announced, then frowned as he took in the strange scene.

"Fido!" said Dooley, then lowered his eyes to the Maine Coon at the man's feet. "Buster!"

"Hey, you guys," said Buster. "Fancy meeting you here!"

"You came back!" said Dooley as we all crowded around our friend.

"Of course!"

"Um… I guess I can come back later?" Fido said.

"I thought you were in California?" said Gran.

"I was, but things didn't work out," said the hair maestro.

"They didn't need hairdressers over there?" asked Odelia with a smile.

"Well, I thought I'd end up with a group of like-minded individuals and work on the future of our planet, only when I got there I discovered that the Flat Earth Society was hopelessly divided. Part of the organization had decided they wanted to ask Elon Musk to drill a hole through the earth so they could prove the earth is flat, while a different section wanted to organize an expedition to the world's end and prove their theories that way. In the end the fighting and the bickering became too much for me, so I decided to chuck the whole thing and come back."

"And now you're working at the hotel?"

"I closed up my shop before I left, and my customers have all left me," he said as he idly played with a comb. "So I just figured I'd start from scratch, and the hotel was the only place that offered to hire me."

"I think you'll find that if you open up that shop of yours again," said Chase, clapping the other man on the back so hard his knees almost buckled, "that your customers will all come flocking back soon enough."

"I'd come back to you," said Gran as she touched her tiny white curls. "In fact I'll come back right now. That hair salon at the mall stinks. They don't know how to do a perfect perm."

"Only you know how I like my hair done, Fido," said Marge.

"Yeah, I missed you, too," said Odelia.

"Just don't mention this flat earth business again, will you?" said Marge. "It's a real turnoff."

"I won't," said Fido with a crooked smile. "I guess I went a little loony there for a while, didn't I?"

"It's that darned internet," said Gran. "It turns everybody looney."

"I know," said Fido. "I watched a YouTube video on how to baste a turkey, and the next video was about how to shoot a turkey, and I don't know how it happened, but suddenly I was watching videos about how the earth is flat, and I couldn't stop! I watched those videos day and night—I had them on autoplay and they just became more and more cuckoo and in the end so did I!"

"That's YouTube for you. You start with a turkey and end up with a cuckoo."

"It's the human brain," said Dooley. "It's a very delicate instrument, and a YouTube bombardment can easily destroy the balance that makes it all work together in perfect harmony."

We all stared at the cat.

Dooley shrugged. "I watch a lot of Discovery Channel. At least it doesn't melt your brain."

A round of heartfelt laughter was his reward, and even Fido laughed, though of course he hadn't understood a word Dooley had said. But the mere fact that three former customers had told him they'd come back in a heartbeat was enough to spirit a big smile onto the hair wizard's face again.

EPILOGUE

Tex had fired up the grill, and had provided the rest of the family with an assortment of sausages, steaks, ribs and other goodies, and the scent of deliciousness had even caused our next-door neighbors Ted and Marcie Trapper to stick their heads over the fence and see where that wonderful smell was coming from. So Tex had very magnanimously invited the couple over, and since the Trappers never went anywhere without their precious sheepdog Rufus, the latter was now lying next to us on the porch, and was chewing at a very large rib. His best friend Fifi, a neighboring Yorkie, had also been invited, and was trying to chew through a piece of steak.

"Tex is definitely improving," said Brutus as he savored the piece of prime beef he'd been fed.

"Yeah, he's improving with leaps and bounds," Harriet agreed as she dug her teeth into a hamburger patty.

"I think it's because he's finally reconciled himself with his position in life," I ventured as I enjoyed the taste of a piece of chicken filet.

"And what is his position in life?" asked Dooley, who was nibbling a meatball.

"Being the town doctor, of course."

We all glanced up at Tex. I still felt a little bad about the way I'd treated him, when all he tried to do was help me get rid of that diamond. Then again, it's hard to control a bowel movement.

"I'm sorry, Tex!" I cried, not for the first time, I might add.

Tex raised his tongs in recognition. Even though my words eluded him, I think he grasped my intention. He'd forgiven me, I like to add, which just shows what a good-hearted man he is.

The rest of the family were all gathered around the table set up in Tex and Marge's backyard, and thoroughly enjoying the feast.

"So what happened to Johnny?" asked Gran.

"Ancient history," said Scarlett with a careless wave of her hand.

"Too attached to his ethically challenged partner?"

"Too needy," Scarlett said as she pronged a potato and bit off a tiny piece. "After our second date he was talking wedding plans. So I told him I don't do marriage, and I don't do cohabitation, and when he kicked up a fuss I kicked him out."

"Good riddance," said Gran.

"Johnny is a nice person," said Marge. "He just hangs out with the wrong crowd."

"He is the wrong crowd," said Gran.

"So what's going on with Loretta?" asked Charlene.

"I was chatting with her last night," said Odelia. "She's in Khemed right now, and things are going great. Bab El Ghat rolled out the red carpet for her and her grandparents and installed them at the palace for the duration of their trip. He wants to make amends, and show them that he's not like his dad. Also, he's asked Loretta to advise him on some necessary changes to the archaic nature of certain Khemed customs. Like polygyny, the right of any man to marry multiple wives."

"Next thing she'll become the Sheikha," said Uncle Alec as he savored his cold beer.

"So who's this Loretta you're talking about?" asked Ted Trapper.

"She's the writer of this fantastic book," said Marge, and handed a copy of The Sheikh's Passion to the Trappers.

Marcie took it and nodded. "I read this. It's great. I saw the other day that Hollywood has bought the rights. They're turning it into a TV series."

"Oh, I wonder who'll play Sheikh Bab El Ehr," said Marge excitedly, "and Loretta's mother."

"I don't care who plays them, as long as they stay true to the book," said Marcie. "Too often they change the whole story and I hate that."

"So how are things with Fido?" asked Uncle Alec.

"He's doing fine. His old customers have all returned," said Marge, nodding. "So all's well that ends well."

"I'm not so sure," said Gran. "When I went in there yesterday he was telling me this whole story about how the earth is actually hollow, and how strange creatures live under our feet."

"Oh, dear," said Marge. "Looks like we'll have to have another talk with him."

"And wean him off the YouTube. For good this time."

"YouTube is overrated," said Brutus. "Tik Tok is where the action is."

I laughed. "Are you into Tik Tok now, Brutus?"

"You bet. Harriet and I made our first Tik Tok movie yesterday. Wanna see?"

"I wouldn't miss it for the world," I said indulgently, as

Harriet fired up the tablet Odelia leaves lying around for us to play with.

Moments later we were all watching a short video of Brutus and Harriet moving to ABBA's Waterloo and doing a funny little dance.

"Cute," said Rufus as he yawned, showing us he wasn't particularly impressed. "But you should see my Tik Tok."

"You have a Tik Tok?" asked Brutus.

"Of course. Me and Fifi made it together," he said.

"We love our Tik Tok, don't we, Rufus?" said Fifi.

"Absolutely. We make a great team." He instructed Harriet to surf to their channel, which was called Ru-Fi, and soon I had to admit Rufus was right: the short videos they'd posted —or that Marcie had posted for them—were fun. They jumped through hoops, played fetch with Ted, and generally did the kind of stuff dogs are good at: basically what their humans told them to do.

"I like Harriet's video better," Dooley whispered in my ear.

"Me, too," I whispered back.

"Why don't we start our own Tik Tok channel, Max? I think it could be a lot of fun."

"Yeah, why not? Odelia can film us and put everything online. But what could we do that would make people watch?"

"I know," said Dooley. "We'll solve mysteries."

"Solve mysteries in under three minutes? That's a stretch, Dooley, even for us."

"Oh, I know, we can dance and shake our tushies, just like Harriet does. People love that stuff."

I arched my eyebrows. Dancing and shaking my tush is not exactly my thing. Then again, if it made my friend happy, why not?

And to show us how it was done, Dooley now hopped

down from the swing, and demonstrated a little dance he'd seen in another Tik Tok video.

We all laughed, and so did the humans, who encouraged Dooley to go on. Then a couple of the humans took out their phones, and soon he was doing a whole show.

"You're a natural, Dooley," said Brutus with a wide grin.

"You should have been a dance star," said Harriet reluctantly. She likes to be the center of attention, and she didn't appreciate sharing the limelight with Dooley.

"Your turn, Max," said Odelia, holding up her phone.

"Yeah, Max," said Gran. "Show us what you got."

"I don't 'got' anything," I said. But since they were cheering me on, I had no alternative but to hop down, and strut my stuff.

Soon we were all dancing to the music, and even Rufus and Fifi joined in, and then it was the humans' turn. And generally a good time was had by all. Even Tex stood shaking and swinging behind his grill, Uncle Alex danced with Charlene, Chase and Odelia demonstrated a few steps of a dance called the tango they'd recently picked up, and Scarlett and Gran showed us they weren't too old to hit the dance floor either. But Ted and Marcie beat us all: they actually danced a mean foxtrot, and moved like professionals!

"YouTube lessons," said Ted, panting when the dance was done. "There's a lot of them, and I mean a *lot*."

Okay, so YouTube can be used for good or for evil, and isn't that the case with all technology? The evening wound down, and it was time to go to bed. At least for the humans. For us cats the night had only just begun. And as we walked along the sidewalk in the direction of the park, a feeling of extreme contentment filled me. "It's nice to have friends, you guys," I suddenly burst out.

"That's your near-death experience talking, buddy," said Brutus.

"What do you mean, near death? I was never near death."

"Oh, yes, you were. If that diamond had slipped a little further down, it would have torn a hole in your gut the size of a melon."

"No way!" Dooley cried. "A whole melon?"

"Yep, a melon, and then you wouldn't be here right now, Max."

"A melon is pretty big, isn't it?" said Dooley.

"Guys, please, let's not talk about gruesome stuff like that," said Harriet.

"If that diamond had been in there five minutes longer," Brutus said, undeterred, "it would have turned Max's insides into mush. Like a blender!"

"No way!" said Dooley. "An actual blender!"

"Yep. Scrambled him up something good."

Friends. You can't live with them—but you can sure live without them, right? Though I have to admit I was still glad to have them.

"If that diamond had been in there for only a single minute more, it would have torn a hole in Max's gut the size of Mount Everest!"

"No way! That's a big hole, Brutus!"

Ugh. See what I mean?

THE END

Thanks for reading! If you want to know when a new Nic Saint book comes out, sign up for Nic's mailing list: nicsaint.com/news

EXCERPT FROM DEATH IN SUBURBIA (THE KELLYS 2)

Chapter One

"Scott! Get up! Time for breakfast!"

Scott groaned, opened one eye and saw that the day had already started without him. He didn't mind. As far as he was concerned, the day could do whatever it wanted. So he closed his eyes again and tried to return to the dream he'd abandoned. The one where he was Han Solo and instead of having to endure that weird hairy ape as a traveling companion he conquered the universe with Emilia Clarke by his side. Now wouldn't *that* be something!

But before he and lovely Emilia could board the Millennium Falcon, Mom's voice pierced the fragile fabric of sleep once more—effectively ending his roseate dreamscape.

"Scott! Out of bed! Now!"

He threw back the comforter, rubbed the sleep from his eyes and yawned. Checking his smartphone, he saw that his best friend Mike was still asleep. If he wasn't he'd have sent him an update on his Pokemon Go conquests from last night. They might be twelve, but that didn't mean Pokemon was beneath them now. Besides, with the new Harry Potter Pokemon coming out soon, they needed to work on their mad skillz.

Shuffling out of his room in the direction of the bathroom, he discovered the door locked. Dragging one hand through his shaggy mane, he pounded the door with the other.

"Go away, scuzz-ball!" his sister yelled from inside.

"You go away, snarf-face!" he yelled back.

"Don't call your sister a snarf-face," said his mother as she hurried past, cradling the baby in her arms.

"Why do you keep carrying Jacob everywhere?" he asked. "He's old enough to walk."

But Mom wasn't listening. Instead, she was pounding down the stairs, still carrying Jacob as if his legs were too weak to carry him. At this rate, the toddler was never going to learn how to walk all by himself. Scott shook his head. Adults. They just never listened.

The door to the bathroom suddenly swung open and Maya appeared, a towel draped around her head and another one around her bony frame. She narrowed her eyes at him. "Why do you need the bathroom anyway? You wear the same grungy shirt three days in a row and you don't even bother to deodorize those pathetic pits of yours."

"I don't need to deodorize my pits," he said, moving past his sister. "My pits naturally smell like roses."

"Nobody's pits smell like roses. Especially yours, little brother."

He squared off against Maya. Even though she was five years older than him, they were the same height. He'd gotten a growth spurt last year to the extent she had no right to call him 'little brother' anymore. "Are you dissing my pits?"

"I'm telling you that if you don't start working on your

personal hygiene no girl is ever going to want to go out with you."

He laughed at this. "Who cares about girls?! All girls are stupid!"

"Have it your own way, freak. I'm just trying to look out for you."

She stomped off, and he plodded into the bathroom and slammed the door.

🕮

Dee heard the door slam and yelled, "Don't slam the door!"

Not that it would do much good. Her kids were at the stage where they'd stopped listening to anything she or Tom said. She remembered just in time not to frown. She was turning forty next year, and she could almost feel the collagen in her face breaking down as that fateful birthday drew closer. Likewise, she tried not to smile too much either, or pucker her lips. She darted a quick look in the hallway mirror. The woman who looked back at her was fair-haired, light-skinned, and quite beautiful. She also had dark rings under her eyes that hadn't been there when she was her lookalike daughter's age. Ugh.

Inadvertently, she'd put Jacob down. The toddler was looking up at her, then gave her a cheerful smile. "Mommy!" he cried, then held out his arms. "Carry!"

Scott's words hadn't missed their effect, though. Her son was right. The days of lugging the little tyke all over the place were over. In Dec's defense, though, she only carried him up and down the stairs these days, and only when she was in a hurry. "Go to the kitchen," she said encouragingly. "Go and find Daddy."

"Daddy!" Jacob said, and lo and behold, he moved off at an awkward wobble in the general direction of the kitchen.

EXCERPT FROM DEATH IN SUBURBIA (THE KELLYS 2)

As she followed him at a little distance, Dee smiled. He was such a lively, cheerful little dude. Never gave his mom and dad any trouble at all. Unlike Scott, who'd been a real cryer, and Maya, who'd been a restless kid. Looked like third time was the charm after all.

Behind her, Ralph came trotting down the stairs, his nails clicking funnily on the steps. The family Goldendoodle was a late riser, too, and proved it by plopping down on his heinie and yawning widely. He then barked once and followed Dee into the kitchen, where he proceeded to hover over his food bowl and give it a tentative sniff before digging in.

Meanwhile Dee's husband of twenty years, Tom Kelly, was juggling a skillet and a glass bowl of pancake batter, creating the perfect morning treat. A pot of coffee stood spreading its wonderful aroma through the kitchen and the table was already set for six. Dee's mom Caroline was presiding over the breakfast nook, preparing the kids' lunches.

"Mom," said Dee as she hoisted Jacob into his seat, "I told you. Maya doesn't need you to pack her a school lunch. She grabs whatever from the cafeteria." Or the Starbucks around the corner.

"I don't mind," said Mom as she added an apple to the lunch box. "Besides, the stuff they offer at schools these days is not healthy. Just a steaming pile of junk food. Unfit for man or beast."

"They have a healthy alternative," she said as she outfitted her youngest with a bib.

"You know kids. When they have a choice between a greasy burger or a plate of veggies they'll take the burger every time. Honestly, Dee, how hard is it to prepare a healthy and nutritious lunch?"

"Not hard at all. Problem is she won't eat it. I can tell you that right now. She'll dump it in the trash first chance she gets."

"No, she won't. Not when her grammy put that extra-special ingredient in there. Love," she explained.

"Love or no love—she'll trash it. Just you wait and see."

Dee's mom stubbornly pursed her lips. "No, she won't. My angel wouldn't do that to a lunch her own grammy packed. Nuh-uh."

Dee wanted to explain that Maya had stopped being an angel a long time ago but decided this was a battle she was never going to win.

"Honey," said her husband, setting down a plate of pancakes. "Can you try one? I have a feeling I forgot to add something but I don't know what it is."

Dee forked a pancake and took a bite. She grimaced. "You forgot the sugar, hon."

"Dang it," Tom murmured. "Knew I'd left something out."

Dee shared a smile with her mother. Tom really was the absent-minded professor incarnate. Not only was he a real-life professor—in economics, not chemistry—but he was as scatterbrained as they came.

"Don't you worry about a thing, Tom," said Mom. "We'll just add more jam." And to show them she meant business, she spooned a generous helping of strawberry jam onto her pancake and transferred it into her mouth. Talk about your healthy alternative.

"Kids!" Tom bellowed at the foot of the stairs. "If you don't get down here right now we're all gonna be late for school!" He darted a quick look at his wife. "And the gallery!"

"I don't know why you keep going to that place," said Mom as she added a granola bar to Scott's lunchbox. "You hired that nice girl—what's-her-name—I wanna say Trixie?"

"Holly," Dee corrected her mother, then tucked a small piece of apple into Jacob's mouth. He happily munched down on it, half the apple soon dribbling down his chin. "And the reason I keep going is because it's my gallery, Mom. I'm the one in charge."

"Sounds to me like this Trixie person is on top of things."

"Holly. And she is on top of things. But I still have to be there to handle stuff like acquisitions, communicating with the artists and collectors, setting up exhibitions…"

Mom was waving her hand. "Trixie can handle all of that stuff." She gestured to Jacob. "What she can't do is take care of your baby. That is something only you can do. Raising your kid. A few short years from now all three of your babies will be gone and that gallery will still be there waiting for you to run it. Not that I mind babysitting my grandchild," she quickly added when Dee opened her mouth to respond. "In fact I love it. But a mother leaving her child at home all day?" She shrugged. "It's just not right."

"Do you think I want to be in Seattle when I could be here at home with Jacob?"

"Oh, I know, sweetie," said her mother, reaching over to pinch her cheek as if she was the toddler, not Jacob. "But actions speak louder than words, so get your priorities straight, all right? And I'm sure Tom will back me up on this —won't you, Tom?"

Tom looked up from his study of the bowl of leftover pancake batter, a confused look on his face. At forty-eight, he actually managed to look younger than his wife, who was almost a decade his junior. How he did this, Dee did not know. "Mh?" said Tom.

"Do you or don't you agree that your wife should be home with her child instead of gallivanting around with a bunch of wannabe artists?" said Mom, enunciating clearly and distinctly as if addressing a three-year-old.

Tom's eyes shifted to Dee. "Um…"

"Oh, for crying out loud," Mom said, throwing up her hands.

"You know, if you want to stay home I'm sure we can arrange something," said Tom. "I mean financially we can definitely manage, so…"

"Look, I love my job, all right? I worked hard to set up that gallery and I can't afford to abandon it when it's still finding its feet. People who visit the Dee Kelly Gallery expect to find Dee Kelly there to greet them, not a salaried second-in-command. Besides, I'm just working mornings right now."

"You're absolutely right," said Tom soothingly, then moved over to peck a quick kiss to her brow.

"Looks like we've been vetoed, little man," said Mom, tucking a piece of pancake into Jacob's mouth.

The toddler happily gobbled up the treat, then cackled loudly. "Want more!" he yelled.

"Looks like we're getting new neighbors," said Scott, slouching into the kitchen, then draping his limp frame across a chair as if he were a bag of bones instead of a real boy.

"New neighbors?" asked Tom. "What do you mean?"

"I mean there's a moving truck backing up the driveway as we speak."

All eyes moved to the window, which offered a great view of the house next door. Scott was right. A truck was backing up the neighboring driveway, two burly movers instructing the driver with word and gesture.

"Huh," said Tom. "I didn't even know the house had been sold."

Maya waltzed into the kitchen, her eyes glued to her smartphone. "You guys, did you know that Gwen Stefani is having another baby? Isn't she, like, a thousand years old or something?"

Tom looked offended. "Gwen Stefani is my age," he said.

"Yeah, well, newsflash, Dad," said Maya. "You're old, too."

"We're getting new neighbors," Scott announced. "I hope they have a dog."

Maya's eyes snapped to the window. "Neighbors?" When she noticed the moving van, her jaw fell. "Are you kidding me right now?" She turned to her mother. "Mom—I told you we should have gotten those curtains up. Now what am I going to do?"

Scott grinned. "Relax, fuzz-face. Nobody's gonna look through your window."

"Shut up. Mom! I need curtains ASAP!"

"A girl needs her privacy," Dee's mom agreed.

"Dad!" Maya cried plaintively. "I can't have a bunch of hormonal teenagers spying on me!"

"You won't, darling," said Tom. "I'll get you those curtains. And you, Scott."

"I don't need no curtains," said Scott, shoving his fifth pancake into his mouth, this one drowning in syrup. "Unlike my sister, I got nothing to hide." Even with his mouth full of pancake, he managed a smirk, earning him a vicious scowl from Maya.

Dee's eyes happened to wander over to the clock on the kitchen wall. When she saw what time it was, she jolted into action. "You guys, we have to get moving. Scott—thank your grandmother for preparing your lunch—you, too, Maya. Chop, chop! Let's go, Kellys!"

Within five minutes, they were all racing for the exit, Dee after giving Baby Jacob a smacking kiss on the sticky cheek and promising her mother she'd be home in a couple of hours. And then they were off, leaving the kitchen a mess and Caroline shaking her head at the hullabaloo a family of five could create.

Dee then stuck her head back in. "Love you, Mom," she said. "Wouldn't know what to do without you."

"Get out of here, you," said Caroline. Then, when Dee directed a dazzling smile at her, added grudgingly, "I love you, too. Now better get going, or Trixie will be pissed."

Chapter Two

Scott took his bike from the garage and waved to Mike, who was staring at the moving van.

"Hey, buddy," said Scott as he rode up to his friend.

"You're getting new neighbors," Mike said, showing his keen powers of observation.

"Yeah. I hope they've got a dog."

"A dog? A girl, you mean."

"Girl? What girl?"

"A girl our age! A girl you can fall in love with—moon over while you're staring out of your window while she's staring out of hers." He'd pressed his hands to his chest and was looking up at the sky. "A girl so pretty you'll write her *poems* and sing her songs of *love*."

Scott eyed his friend with an expression of abject horror on his freckled face. "Are you crazy? Who needs girls?!"

"We do," said Mike as he craned his neck to catch a glimpse of whoever was moving in next door.

It shouldn't have surprised Scott that his friend felt this way. Mike was something of a dork. With his braces and his glasses he looked like one, too. Not that it bothered Scott. Mike had been his buddy ever since the Kellys moved from Medina to Issaquah where they now lived. Changing neighborhoods had been tough, but not as tough as changing schools. Making new friends had been an iffy proposition at first, and it was only when he and Mike had bonded over their shared ability to squirt orange juice out of their noses that things had started looking up again. Now they were inseparable.

"I like girls," Mike said reverently. "I like Maggie Cooper."
"Who's Maggie Cooper?"
"She's only the prettiest girl in school. Hair like spun gold. Eyes like Alaskan lakes. A nose like…" He frowned, his poetic prowess momentarily deserting him. "A nose like, um…"

"Yeah, yeah. I get the picture," said Scott, who, unlike Mike, didn't worship at the feet of girls—even if their hair was like spun gold—whatever spun gold was. "Let's get going, buddy. We're gonna be late."

As they rode off on their bikes, the two friends briefly looked back, Mike to see if his friend had just acquired a girl-next-door who could melt his barnacled heart, and Scott to try and catch a glimpse of the dog he hoped these mysterious new neighbors had brought.

Maya's boyfriend was already sitting in his Ford Mustang, parked at the curb, the motor rumbling impressively. The car was a junker Mark's dad had gotten him for his sixteenth birthday but it still worked fine enough. Mark had painted it bright orange with pink stripes in deference to Maya, knowing they were her favorite colors. Maya owned her own car, a pink Mini Cooper, but Mark refused to be seen dead in the thing. Apart from that minor character flaw, the stocky Mark Dean, self-proclaimed football jock, was a surprisingly kind-hearted soul. And as the son of a lumber mill tycoon, he was also comfortably well-off. Not that that mattered a great deal to Maya, whose dad wasn't exactly a pauper either.

"You've got new neighbors," said Mark as Maya slid into the seat.

"Yeah—I hope they're nice. Not like the ones we had in Medina."

The house where they'd lived had been partially blown up

in a home invasion gone wrong. Luckily the Kelly clan had escaped the ordeal unscathed, but they'd still opted to sell the house and relocate to a part of town that wouldn't be a constant reminder of that fateful night.

"Those home invaders weren't neighbors, though, right?"

"Not technically," she admitted. The leader of the gang had been a Seattle mobster. Not a neighbor, per se, but close enough. "Let's not talk about that, Mark."

He gave her a rueful look. "I'm sorry. I won't mention it again."

Strictly speaking, she'd been the one to dredge up the wretched past, but watching Mark's expression of contrition was too much fun. She placed a hand on his cheek. "That's all right, Mark. You can always make it up to me."

His face lit up with a goofy grin. "That's more like it. Anything you want, babe."

She grimaced. "First off, don't call me babe. I hate it. Second, you can start by driving me to school. We're going to be late."

"What happened to your car?"

"Being serviced. Engine trouble." In actual fact she'd scratched the paint by hitting the mailbox last night, but she wasn't going to give Mark a reason to mock her driving skills.

Dad had bought her the car because school was now a respectable distance from her house, owing to the fact that she'd opted to stay in the same school as before, when they were still living in Medina. Seeing as she only had one more year of high school to go, it would have been a shame to switch schools like her little brother had done. One more year and she was off to college—the same university where her dad taught: the University of Washington, also known as U-Dub.

"So have you thought about filling out that college application?" she asked Mark as he eased the car away from the curb.

"Um…"

She rolled her eyes. "Mark! You promised!"

"The thing is… my dad keeps talking retirement. I don't want to let the old man down."

"Your dad has been talking retirement since he took over from his dad." She tucked a lock of blond hair behind her ear. "You know you'll be able to take that company and launch it into the stratosphere if you get an economics degree, right? My dad explained all that to you."

"I know, babe. It's just that… my grades just aren't that great."

She knew what he meant. Mark was a sweetheart, and a great athlete. What he wasn't was academically gifted. "I'm sure with a little help from me and my dad you'll do just fine. Remember, you don't have to graduate at the top of your class, Mark. You just have to graduate, period."

He emitted a noncommittal sound, then focused on the road. She gritted her teeth in disappointment. He was going to take his dad's advice and take over the lumber mill, wasn't he? Who needs a college education when you've got a perfectly good job waiting for you? And his dad had been talking retirement mainly because the Seattle weather was wreaking havoc on his arthritic joints and he was dreaming of becoming a snowbird.

What she didn't want to admit was the real reason she wanted Mark to join her at UW: the fact that she feared drifting apart if he were to join his family company while she became a college student. She punched his shoulder.

"Ow! What did you do that for?" he said.

She punched his shoulder again, harder this time.

"Hey! That's my good arm. I need that arm."

She gave him another few light punches.

"You punch like a girl," he chuckled.

"That's probably because I am a girl."

He gave her a quick sideways glance. "Are you all right?"

She did the eye roll thing again. "What do you think?"

He narrowed his eyes. "Is it that time of the month again?"

She raised her fist to give him her biggest punch yet but by now he was laughing so hard she decided not to bother. "You know what, Mark? If you don't want to go to college with me just say so. Don't give me this lame excuse of your dad says this and your dad says that."

"But my dad really says all those things!"

"Ugh," she said, and settled down in her seat, her arms folded across her chest.

"I want to go to college with you, babe," he said finally. "It's just that… I don't think I'm smart enough, okay?"

She looked up, surprised. "What are you talking about?"

"Your dad—he's like, a genius, okay? But every time he talks shop, my eyes glaze over. I don't understand a word he's saying! So I figure four years of that is going to kill me—if I ever make it that far in the first place. I'm not college material, babe—I'm just not!"

She was touched by the vulnerability he displayed. It was a side of him he rarely showed. "I'm sure that with a little tutoring from my dad—"

"But that's just it. I listen to the guy and I blank out. Completely! It's like listening to Coach Martin when he's trying to introduce a new running play. I'm not smart that way. I need to see something with my own eyes—go through the motions a couple times before I get it. And this economics gobbledygook is just… gobbledygook!"

She grinned. She got it now, and patted him on the shoulder. "Don't you worry about a thing. Just follow my lead and you'll make it through four years of gobbledygook just fine."

Now that she knew what ailed him, she knew exactly what to do about it, too.

He gave her a curious glance. "Uh-oh," he said. "I know that look."

"What look?"

"You've got some kind of plan, don't you?"

"Of course I've got a plan. Never go through life without a plan. Isn't that what I keep telling you?"

He gave her a lost-puppy look. "Uh-huh," he said tentatively.

She patted his shoulder again. "I've got this," she assured him.

"That's what I'm afraid of," he murmured.

Chapter Three

As Tom drove the family Toyota Sienna out of the driveway he stared so hard at the moving van he almost clipped the mailbox.

"Watch out!" Dee cried.

He stomped on the brake and the car screeched to a standstill. "I wonder who they are," he said as he eased the car into reverse and backed up. "First thing tonight let's go over and introduce ourselves." Already he was painting a mental picture of their new neighbor. A professor, just like himself—possibly in a less technical field. Archeology? Or something really cool like robotics or artificial intelligence? They could chat over the hedge—exchange ideas while their wives socialized over preprandial martinis on the patio. Or he could show his new neighbor his newly acquired collection of model trains and tracks.

In his mind's eye he was already picturing himself and this kindly man who was a few years his senior rolling up their collective sleeves and constructing a train track in their combined backyards, just like Walt Disney did back in the day. Wouldn't that be something?

"Do you want me to drive, honey?" asked his wife, giving him a worried look.

"Mh? Oh, no, I'm fine. Just wondering... Do people still bring over a freshly baked pie? Or is that too old-fashioned?"

"We can bring a pie," said Dee. "Or a bottle of wine. Just not sure if they're..."

"The pie-eating or the wine-drinking kind of people," Tom finished the sentence. "Gotcha. Probably we should—"

"—spy out who they are before we commit ourselves to one or the other."

Now they were both staring, as Tom drove the car at a snail's pace past the neighboring house.

"I don't see anyone," said Tom. "Maybe they sent the movers ahead of them."

"Or maybe it's Brad Pitt and he'll move in under the cloak of darkness and we'll never get to see him as he'll be coming and going through a secret passageway in the basement."

Tom gave his wife a curious look. "Brad Pitt? Really?"

"I wouldn't mind if Angelina Jolie moved in so you can't mind if Brad Pitt moves in."

"You do know that Brangelina is no more, right?"

"Of course I know. Brad is single now," she said with a touch of wistfulness.

They stared some more. "I just hope they're nice people," said Tom. With a keen interest in model trains who didn't mind getting their hands dirty while laying track.

"And I hope they have a boy Scott's age and a girl Maya's age and the kids can bond."

"Don't forget a dog who's Ralph's age and a baby Jacob's age."

He touched his foot down on the accelerator and soon they were cruising through the neighborhood, which consisted entirely of similar houses to their own. After last year's home invasion, the Kelly family mantra was not to stand out, and stand out they definitely did not. They drove a nice sensible family car, occupied a nice sensible single-family home, and lived a nice sensible family life. Nothing to see here, folks. Move right along!

After he'd dropped off his wife at the art gallery, Tom proceeded towards his own place of business, the university he called his home away from home. Breezing into his office, he plunked down his floppy brown leather satchel, drew a hand through his floppy brown hair and dropped down in his swivel chair, booting up his computer as he did. Before he had a chance to check his schedule, a knock on the door alerted him of his first visitor.

"Come in!" he boomed.

The door opened and a head poked in. The head was pale and festooned with red spots, the few remaining hairs on the top awkwardly combed to cover the acreage.

"Hey, Tom," said Elliott Lusky, head of the history department.

"Elliott," said Tom jovially. "So have you thought about my offer?"

Elliott shook his bulbous head mournfully. "No can do, I'm afraid. The wife has been nagging me to take her on one of those Alaskan cruises and she's earmarked every last penny in our savings account for that particular purpose. Terribly inconvenient, I know."

Tom leaned back in his chair. "Can't you tell her you're allergic to Alaska or something?" Ever since Tom had seen a documentary about Walt Disney's love for model trains he'd been dreaming of building his own, smaller version of the impressive set Uncle Walt had built in his backyard in the fifties. To this end he needed allies—friends he could share his new passion with. And Elliott was just such a friend. Unfortunately the tubby little man was displaying an awful lot of sales resistance.

"I'm afraid not," said Elliott with a look of apology on his face. "She wanted to go last year. I managed to stave off the disaster by claiming Alaska was in fact part of Canada and we'd need a visa, which we'd never get as I've been declared persona non grata in Canuck country ever since I got drunk and disorderly on a high school trip to Montreal."

"You don't need a visa to visit Canada."

"I know that. The point is that Esther doesn't—or didn't." He frowned. "Curse the internet. Not only does she know I lied to her about Alaska being a part of Canada, she's starting to suspect I made up that whole thing about being arrested in Montreal."

"Were you ever arrested in Montreal?"

Tom's colleague rearranged his features into an appropriate expression of contrition. "No, I was not. An exceedingly nice police officer once cautioned me for jaywalking, though."

"I don't think that counts."

"I don't think so either. Anyway, as it stands she's already booked the tickets so it looks like I'm in for it. I'll have to traipse along while she watches humpback whales cavort in the surf or glides down one of those wretched glaciers."

"Do people actually glide down glaciers? I would have thought that was dangerous. People have been known to tumble down a crevasse never to be seen again."

A gleam of hope lit up the distinguished history professor's face. But then he shook his head, the gleam extinguished. "With my luck that will never happen." He checked his watch. "Have to run, Tom. I've got a class to teach on the

Borgia family." He stared before him for a moment. "They were very fond of arsenic, those Borgias. Liked to poison their husbands. And their wives. Excruciatingly painful, death by arsenic. Very effective."

And with these words he held up his hand and withdrew, gently closing the door.

ABOUT NIC

Nic has a background in political science and before being struck by the writing bug worked odd jobs around the world (including but not limited to massage therapist in Mexico, gardener in Italy, restaurant manager in India, and Berlitz teacher in Belgium).

When he's not writing he enjoys curling up with a good (comic) book, watching British crime dramas, French comedies or Nancy Meyers movies, sampling pastry (apple cake!), pasta and chocolate (preferably the dark variety), twisting himself into a pretzel doing morning yoga, going for a run, and spoiling his big red tomcat Tommy.

He lives with his wife (and aforementioned cat) in a small village smack dab in the middle of absolutely nowhere and is probably writing his next 'Mysteries of Max' book right now.

www.nicsaint.com

ALSO BY NIC SAINT

The Mysteries of Max
Purrfect Murder
Purrfectly Deadly
Purrfect Revenge
Purrfect Heat
Purrfect Crime
Purrfect Rivalry
Purrfect Peril
Purrfect Secret
Purrfect Alibi
Purrfect Obsession
Purrfect Betrayal
Purrfectly Clueless
Purrfectly Royal
Purrfect Cut
Purrfect Trap
Purrfectly Hidden
Purrfect Kill
Purrfect Boy Toy
Purrfectly Dogged
Purrfectly Dead
Purrfect Saint
Purrfect Advice
Purrfect Cover

Purrfect Patsy
Purrfect Son
Purrfect Fool
Purrfect Fitness
Purrfect Setup
Purrfect Sidekick
Purrfect Deceit
Purrfect Ruse
Purrfect Swing
Purrfect Cruise
Purrfect Harmony
Purrfect Sparkle

The Mysteries of Max Box Sets
Box Set 1 (Books 1-3)
Box Set 2 (Books 4-6)
Box Set 3 (Books 7-9)
Box Set 4 (Books 10-12)
Box Set 5 (Books 13-15)
Box Set 6 (Books 16-18)
Box Set 7 (Books 19-21)
Box Set 8 (Books 22-24)
Box Set 9 (Books 25-27)
Box Set 10 (Books 28-30)
Box Set 11 (Books 31-33)

The Mysteries of Max Shorts
Purrfect Santa (3 shorts in one)
Purrfectly Flealess

Purrfect Wedding

Nora Steel

Murder Retreat

The Kellys

Murder Motel

Death in Suburbia

Emily Stone

Murder at the Art Class

Washington & Jefferson

First Shot

Alice Whitehouse

Spooky Times

Spooky Trills

Spooky End

Spooky Spells

Ghosts of London

Between a Ghost and a Spooky Place

Public Ghost Number One

Ghost Save the Queen

Box Set 1 (Books 1-3)

A Tale of Two Harrys

Ghost of Girlband Past

Ghostlier Things

Charleneland

Deadly Ride

Final Ride

Neighborhood Witch Committee

Witchy Start

Witchy Worries

Witchy Wishes

Saffron Diffley

Crime and Retribution

Vice and Verdict

Felonies and Penalties (Saffron Diffley Short 1)

The B-Team

Once Upon a Spy

Tate-à-Tate

Enemy of the Tates

Ghosts vs. Spies

The Ghost Who Came in from the Cold

Witchy Fingers

Witchy Trouble

Witchy Hexations

Witchy Possessions

Witchy Riches

Box Set 1 (Books 1-4)

The Mysteries of Bell & Whitehouse

One Spoonful of Trouble

Two Scoops of Murder
Three Shots of Disaster
Box Set 1 (Books 1-3)
A Twist of Wraith
A Touch of Ghost
A Clash of Spooks
Box Set 2 (Books 4-6)
The Stuffing of Nightmares
A Breath of Dead Air
An Act of Hodd
Box Set 3 (Books 7-9)
A Game of Dons

Standalone Novels
When in Bruges
The Whiskered Spy

ThrillFix
Homejacking
The Eighth Billionaire
The Wrong Woman

Printed in Great Britain
by Amazon